Author Note

Royal wedding! Even the words sound magical.

Unlike Cinderella, however, most royal brides enter marriage as an alliance of state, not of the heart. There are exceptions, and two of the most intriguing were those of the children of Edward III, the fourteenth-century English king. His eldest son and his eldest daughter were both allowed to marry for love—unheard of for a royal at that time, and for centuries after.

This book and my next, *Whispers at Court,* are set in the world surrounding those weddings, where the real drama happens behind the scenes. For the bride of the Black Prince has secrets to keep—secrets her longtime companion Anne must be certain that Sir Nicholas Lovayne never discovers....

Secrets at Court

Blythe Gifford

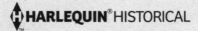

Recycling programs
for this product may
not exist in your area.

ISBN-13: 978-0-373-29777-1

SECRETS AT COURT

Copyright © 2014 by Wendy B. Gifford

Printed in U.S.A.

Available from Harlequin® Historical and
BLYTHE GIFFORD

Did you know that these novels are also available as ebooks? Visit www.Harlequin.com.

Dedication

To all those struggling to move beyond the past.

Acknowledgments

With thanks for the support of the Hermits
and the Hussies, two of my favorite writing tribes.

BLYTHE GIFFORD

After many years in public relations, advertising and marketing, Blythe Gifford started writing seriously after a corporate layoff. Ten years and one layoff later she became an overnight success when she sold her Romance Writers of America Golden Heart finalist manuscript to Harlequin. Her books, set in medieval England or early Tudor Scotland, usually feature a direct connection to historical royalty. *The Chicago Tribune* has called her work "the perfect balance between history and romance". She lives and works along Chicago's lakefront and juggles writing with a consulting career. She loves to have visitors at www.blythegifford.com, "thumbs up" at www.facebook.com/BlytheGifford and "tweets" at www.twitter.com/BlytheGifford.

Chapter One

Windsor Castle—late March, 1361

'Come. Quickly.' A whisper, urgent. Disturbing her dreams.

Anne felt a hand, squeezing her shoulder. She opened her eyes, blinking, to see the Countess holding a candle and leaning over her in the darkness.

Closing her eyes, Anne rolled onto her side. She only dreamt. Lady Joan would never rise in the dead of night. That was left to Anne.

Slender fingers pinched her cheek. 'Are you awake, Anne?'

Suddenly, she was. Throwing back her bedclothes. Reaching for something to cover her feet. 'What is it?' Had the pestilence found them? Or perhaps the French? 'What is the hour?'

Lady Joan waved a hand. 'Dark.' Then, she gripped Anne's fingers and tugged. 'Come. I need you.'

Anne tried to stand. Awkward, more out of balance than usual. She patted the sheets, searching for her walking stick.

'Here.' It was thrust into her hand. Then, the Countess, putting her impatience aside, offered a shoulder to help Anne rise.

Kindness from her lady, often when it was least expected. Or wanted.

Walking staff tucked snugly under her left arm, Anne hobbled through Windsor's corridors, mindful that Lady Joan had put a finger to her lips to signal quiet and gestured for her to hurry. As if Anne had any control over either. Between stick and stairs, she could not hurry unless she wanted to tumble to the bottom and risk her only good leg in the process.

Lady Joan led her toward the royal quarters and into an echoing chapel, dark except for a candle, held by someone standing before the altar. A man, tall and strong.

Edward of Woodstock, eldest son of the King, Prince of England, smiling and looking nothing like the stern warrior she, nay, all England and France knew.

Lady Joan was beaming, too. No longer sparing a glance for Anne, she moved swiftly to join her hand with his. 'Here. Now. With a witness.'

No. It could not be what she intended. But Lady Joan, of all people, knew what must be done and how important a witness would be.

The Prince took her candle and set them both on the trestle that served as an altar. Wavering flames cast shadows upwards on their faces, throwing the

Prince's nose and cheekbones into sharp relief and softening her lady's rounded smile. Then they clasped hands, fingers tight, one on top of the other's.

'I, Edward, take thee, Joan, to be my wedded wife.'

Anne swallowed, speechless. Surely God must want her to speak, to prevent this sacrilege?

'Thee to love and keep, as a man ought to love his wife…'

She freed her voice. 'You mustn't. You cannot! The King, you are too close…'

The Prince's scowl stopped her speech. They knew the truth better than she. They shared a royal grandfather, a connection too close for the church to allow this marriage.

'All will be as it must,' Lady Joan said. 'As soon as we have said the vows, we will send a petition to the Pope. He will set aside the impediment and then we will be wed in the church.'

'But…' Anne let the objections fade. The Countess believed it would be as easy as that. Logic, reason, all for naught. Lady Joan would do as she pleased and the world would accommodate her.

It had ever been thus.

The Prince withdrew his frown and faced his bride again. '…and thereto, I plight thee my troth.'

As if he knew exactly the words to say.

Ah, but her lady knew. Lady Joan knew *exactly* what must be done to make such a marriage valid.

Now, she heard her lady's voice, the soft, seductive tone Anne knew too well. 'I, Joan, take thee, Edward, to be my wedded husband…'

Intentions stated, clearly. Too late to protest now.

The chill of the midnight chapel sank into her bones. She would be the one. She would be the one who held the truth of Lady Joan's clandestine marriage.

Again.

Within sight of the English coast—four months later

The waters of the channel pitched and rolled less than usual this day, if Nicholas's stomach was any judge. The tide was with them. He would be ashore by midday and at Windsor Castle before week's end, his duty discharged.

Free of responsibility.

He was weary of his duty. A moment unheeded and the horses you held in reserve would go lame, victuals would be lost, or hail would fall out of a spring sky, destroying food, armour, men and the decisive victory the King had sought for twenty years.

'Sir?'

He turned from seeking the shoreline to look at his squire, Eustace. The boy had hardened on this journey.

He was not the only one. 'Yes?'

'Your things are packed. All is ready.'

There was a question at the end of the sentence. 'Except?'

'Except your horse.'

He sighed. Horses were meant for land, not water. Without a word, he left the sharp, bracing air of the deck and descended to the cramped, smelly bowels of the ship.

No wonder the horse was ill. If he had been confined to this cesspool, he would be, too.

The horse's head hung low, nearly touching the floor. Unable to throw out the contents of his belly as a man would do, the poor beast could only stand, miserable, shedding tears and sweat like rain.

Nicholas stroked his neck and the animal, barely able to lift his head, seemed to open his eyes and blink in gratitude.

No. He would not ride this horse today. The final miles of this journey stretched before him, as difficult as all the rest had been.

But the Edwards, both King and Prince, would have no patience for excuses. Princes and popes need only speak a thing for it to happen, expecting mere mortals such as Nicholas Lovayne to create the needed miracles.

And time after time, he did. He made certain there was always an alternate route, always another choice, always one more way the goal might be reached, never exhausting the possibilities until the deed was done.

There was pride in that.

But his other horse had succumbed on this journey, so he would find another way.

Leaving his squire to unload, Nicholas disembarked and was greeted by the warden of the Cinque Ports. He, too, had ridden with the Prince in France, though Nicholas did not know him well. It did not matter. Men who had shared a war all knew each other. A horse would be provided.

'What news in my absence?' Nicholas asked. It had taken near six weeks to travel to Avignon and back. Time enough for three intrigues and more to swirl about the court. He must prepare for this as he would prepare for a battle, knowing how the ground lay and where the troops massed.

'Pestilence still stalks the land.'

More than ten years since the last time. He had thought, they all had, that God's punishment was behind them.

'The King. Is he at Windsor?'

The warden shook his head. 'He's closed the courts, suspended the business of the exchequer so men do not need to travel and fled to the New Forest.'

The New Forest. A longer ride, then. Pray God he'd find no pestilence along the way.

'How fares Prince Edward?'

The warden shrugged. 'He is a Prince, not a King. With the war over, he has little to do but cavort with his friends and with the Virgin of Kent.'

Nicholas shot him a sharp look. Few were brave enough to speak so pointedly about Edward's intended.

'And you?' The warden looked at him with open curiosity. 'Was your journey successful?'

Did the entire country know why he'd been sent? Well, he would not speak of it to anyone until he had seen the Prince. The besotted Prince who, instead of making an alliance with a bride from Spain or the Low Countries, had thrown it all away for love of a woman forbidden to him by the laws of the church and common sense.

'I can only say,' he spoke carefully, 'that it will not go well with me if it did not.'

For Prince Edward had expected him to obtain the Pope's blessing of a folly too foolish to be forgiven.

And Nicholas was a man who did not suffer fools. Even royal ones.

A lodge in the New Forest—a few days later

After all these years, Anne sometimes tried to run, as she did in dreams. Run as other women her age might, happily chasing their children, playing peek and hide.

Instead, her gait was an awkward, rolling thing. Even when she walked, she rose and sank as if she were a drunken sailor on a tottering ship. The walking stick, a third leg to compensate for the useless second one, only made things more difficult. Sometimes, she tripped over her lame foot and could not withhold her curses, and when she fell, she had learned that rolling would soften the blow.

She had stumbled when the King's ambassador arrived, but fortunately out of his sight and hearing. Tall and straight, he swung off his horse and strode into the keep, his very ease mocking her.

Poor, foolish Anne. Still longing for a body other than the one she had been born with.

She paused before her lady's chamber, gasping for breath, then pushed open the door without knocking for permission.

Even that rude entry could not disturb Lady Joan's perpetual smile. Anne's news, however, would. 'The emissary. He has returned.'

The smile tightened, as if pulled by a vice. They exchanged a wordless glance. 'Have him come to me first.'

Anne held back a retort. Did the woman think to change the news if it were not to her liking? 'But the King—'

'Yes. Of course. The King will want to see him immediately.' She rose. 'I must find Edward.'

Anne sighed. Joan would find her 'husband' and, if the news were bad, she would hear it together with him for the last moments she could call him so.

'And, Anne…' She raised her eyebrows. Not a question. A warning.

'As ever, my lady.'

The beautiful face relaxed into its accustomed smile. She took a breath. 'All will be as it must.'

Anne waited until her lady had turned away before she looked to Heaven for patience. 'As it must' meant as her lady wished it.

She trailed her mistress out of the door, but there was no need to search for Prince Edward. He had already come, as if he had known her need. He took her in his arms, kissed her brow, murmured in her ear, as if no one were near to see.

Anne pursed her lips, fighting a wave of pain. Not in her leg, no. That was perpetual, comforting in its faithfulness. This was different. This was the pain of knowing that no one would ever look at her that way.

Forgive my ingratitude. Her perpetual prayer.

She had no reason to complain. Her mother had assured her future at an early age, saving Anne from a certain fate of begging beside the road. Instead, she was a lady-in-waiting to a woman who, if today's news were good, would one day take her place beside England's King.

Yet as her mistress and the Prince kissed, Anne looked on them with blatant envy. It was not Edward of Woodstock she coveted. For all his glory, he was not a man who appealed to her. She merely wished that a man might smile, his face aglow, just to see her.

As it was, she was clever and unobtrusive and had a face most men did not care to dwell on, so if her expression ever slipped, which it often did, no one would be watching.

They did not watch now, the Prince and her lady, as they turned toward the King's chambers.

'Milady, shall I…?'

Without bothering to turn, Lady Joan shook her head and waved a hand in dismissal. And as the two walked off together to learn their fate, Anne stood in the hall, alone.

Later, then. Later she would discover whether the Pope had been convinced and all was as it must be.

There was a great deal to be made right. And the man who brought the news had not been smiling.

Nicholas, they had called him.

Sir Nicholas Lovayne had rehearsed his speech during the whole of the ride from the port to the New

Forest astride a borrowed horse. Time enough and more to get the words right.

He was grateful he had, for the minute he arrived, they ushered him into the King's private chambers and he faced the King, the Queen, Prince Edward and Joan, Countess of Kent.

There was no more time to rearrange words.

'Well?' King Edward himself spoke, eyes as piercing as a falcon's. Beside him, the Queen gripped his hand.

Nicholas looked at Prince Edward and Lady Joan, for their lives were the ones at stake. 'They will not be excommunicated for violating the Church's marriage laws.'

The Pope had had every right to do so, but Nicholas and some well-placed gold florins had saved their immortal souls. No small feat and more than they deserved.

Thus was the privilege of royalty. To be rewarded for behaviour that would damn any other mortal.

But that was only the first of the miracles Nicholas had accomplished in Avignon. And not even the one the Prince cared most to hear.

'But we will be allowed to marry?' The Prince, as eager as a boy waiting for his first bedding, though he and his 'bride' had been sharing the sheets for months.

'Yes.' In the best of circumstances, the couple would have needed the Pope's permission to wed, since they were closely related. But they had made the situation much, much worse, by marrying in secret.

Then they had dumped their sins in Nicholas's lap, expecting him to untangle the mess to their satisfaction. 'His Holiness will overlook your consanguinity and also set aside your clandestine marriage. You will be allowed to wed in a church-sanctioned union.'

Allowed to marry and share their lives. And the throne.

Relief. The hard, silent expressions melted. Eyes, lips, shoulders, tongues let loose. How quickly? How soon?

He raised his voice to answer with a tone of caution. 'Also,' he added, 'His Holiness requires that each of you build and endow a chapel.'

Neither the Prince nor the Lady Joan bothered to respond to what would be a minor inconvenience. Instead, Prince Edward held out his hand. 'The document.' A demand. 'Give it to me.'

'It will be sent directly to the Archbishop of Canterbury. I expect he will receive it near Michaelmas. Until then, you must live separately.'

The Prince and his lady turned their eyes on him, as if he, instead of the Pope, had forbidden them their bed. As if two months apart were a lifetime.

Well, that was not the worst of it. 'And there is one more thing,' he said.

Hard silence fell again. They quieted, knowing he had more news to deliver and that it would not be as pleasant as the last.

'What?' The King, of course. He would ever be allowed to speak first. 'What more?'

'A private message will accompany the document. His Holiness asked that I tell you what it will contain.'

It took only a glance from the King. The few attendants with them withdrew, leaving him alone with the royal family.

'Go on,' the King said.

'Before they marry,' Nicholas began, 'His Holiness requires…' Now for the words he had rehearsed. 'The Lady Joan's marriage to Salisbury was annulled.'

The Prince frowned. 'Years ago. That is ancient history.'

Nicholas glanced at Joan, amazed to see her half smile unshaken. 'But it was annulled,' he continued, 'when a previous, secret marriage was upheld.'

'All here are aware of my past,' the lady said.

The King and Queen exchanged glances. Everyone in England was aware of Joan's past. It had not made the Prince's case for marriage any easier.

Nicholas gritted his teeth. There was no easy way to say what he must. 'Lady Joan, you were once married to two men, one of whom still lives.' He saw a flush on her cheek. 'His Holiness asks that before your marriage to the Prince proceeds, an investigation be conducted in the matter of your previous marriage.'

'Why?' It was the Prince who asked, blinded by love to the obvious.

'To be sure,' Nicholas said, unable to keep the irritation from his voice, 'that all was in order.'

The Prince stepped toward him, fists raised, and for a moment Nicholas thought the man would, indeed, punish him for the news he brought. 'You dare imply—'

The King stayed his hand. 'Sir Nicholas is not the one who asks for the enquiry.'

Spared, Nicholas waited until the Prince folded his fists into his elbows, then continued. 'I am bringing this news to you ahead of the Pope's official notice so that you may have time to prepare.'

The Lady Joan's smile never wavered. Her face was so lovely you did not bother to wonder what lay behind it. 'So that when the Pope's official decree arrives, we can wed immediately.' She turned to the Prince. 'He does us a kindness. The matter is easily resolved.'

So the Pope expected, Nicholas was certain. His dispensation would arrive in little more than two months, scarcely time to conduct a thorough investigation.

Lady Joan turned her smile on Nicholas. 'All was done correctly in the nullification of my marriage to Salisbury.'

Most women would never have risked a clandestine marriage. This woman had dared two. Her first, to Thomas Holland, twenty-one years ago, was ultimately validated. As a result, she was allowed to put aside her subsequent union with Salisbury and return to Holland instead.

All enough to confuse even the most learned of church scholars.

'His Holiness is not only interested in that one,' Nicholas said, dreading what would come next.

They stared at him as if he had spoken Greek.

'What do you mean?' Lady Joan's voice had an edge he had not heard before.

Obviously, they had not grasped the full meaning of the message. 'He wants more than the nullification investigated. He wants confirmation of the legitimacy of your secret union with Holland.'

Her eyes widened and narrowed. A woman unaccustomed to being questioned, even to prove something as simple as what had already been blessed by a previous pope. 'I don't understand. The Pope, all his people…it took years, but they were satisfied. Surely there could be no question now.'

'A formality, no doubt.' The King, near as adept at government as he was at war. 'The Archbishop will assemble a panel of bishops. They will review the documents. It will be done.'

'The Archbishop is in his seventh decade,' the Prince snapped. 'I doubt he can even find the documents, let alone read them.'

'If not,' Nicholas said, 'perhaps he could question those involved.'

For the first time, Joan's lips tightened and he could see the fine lines radiating from them like the rays of the sun. The woman was, after all, beyond thirty. 'My husband is dead. There is no one to question but me.'

No witnesses, of course. The very definition of a clandestine marriage was that the participants made their vows to each other alone. But there must be other ways. There always were. 'Perhaps someone remembers the two of you together at that time.' Perhaps someone witnessed the Lady Joan and Thomas Holland kissing in corners.

He looked to the Queen, trying to assess her thoughts. The young Joan had been part of her household back then, near a daughter. Awkward, but they had been through this before. The Queen, no doubt, could satisfy any questions.

Fortunately, it would not be his concern. He had delivered his message. By next week, he would be on his way to France, with no responsibility other than to stay alive.

'I don't understand,' Lady Joan said, looking at the Prince as if he might save her. 'What can be the purpose of this?'

Queen Philippa leaned over to pat her hand. 'There must be no question.'

'Question about what?' The Countess, plaintive as a child. And as naïve.

Did love make everyone so? All the better that he refrained.

The Queen looked at her husband, then back. 'About the children.'

There must be no question that the Prince and his bride were married in the sight of God and that their children would be legitimate, with free and clear rights to the throne of England. If a woman over thirty were still fertile enough for children.

Lady Joan coloured and her lips thinned. 'I see. Of course.'

The Prince took her other hand and tucked it

against his side. Still a mystery, to see this man of war smile like a silly child when he gazed at this woman. 'Nicholas will conduct the investigation himself.'

No. He was weary of carrying burdens for others.

He had worked his last earthly miracle. He wanted only to be a fighting man whose sole duty was to survive, not to conjure horses or wine or papal dispensations. 'Your Grace agreed that there would be no more—'

But the King's expression closed that option. 'Until they are wed, your task is undone.'

Nicholas swallowed a retort and nodded, curtly, wondering whether the King had wanted him to succeed so completely. There had been other women, other alliances, that would have suited England's purposes better than this one. 'Of course, your Grace.' A few more weeks, then. All because some clerk in the Pope's retinue wanted an excuse to extract a final florin. 'I shall leave for Canterbury tomorrow to meet with the Archbishop.'

The Prince looked at Nicholas, all trace of the smile gone. 'I shall ride with you.'

Chapter Two

Usually, Lady Joan floated into a room and settled on to her seat as lightly as a bird alighting on a branch.

Not today. Had the news not been to her liking?

'What is wrong, my lady?' Anne bit her tongue. She should not have spoken so bluntly.

The Countess was rarely irous. When she was, Anne knew how to coax her with warm scented water for her hands and her temples, with a hot fire in winter or an offer to bring out her latest bauble to distract and delight her eye. If that did not work, she would summon Robert the Fool to juggle and tumble about the room. Sometimes, if they were clean and not crying, seeing her children could restore the balance of her humour.

Normally, her mistress buried all beneath a smile and behind eyes that gazed adoringly at the man before her. But today...

Anne put aside her stitching as her lady paced the

room like a skittish horse. Then, she remembered the ambassador's face. The news must not have been all Lady Joan wanted. 'The decision of the Pope? Will you and the Prince be allowed…?'

'Yes, yes. But first, they think to investigate my clandestine marriage.'

Relieved, Anne picked up her needle. Well, thus was the reason she had been roused from her bed in the middle of the night. 'I witnessed it, of course. And will tell them so.'

The large blue eyes turned on her. 'Not that one.'

Her hands stopped making stitches and she swallowed. 'What? To what purpose? You have no enemies.'

Lady Joan laughed, that lovely sound that captivated so many. 'Even our friends find it difficult to countenance the marriage of the Prince to an English widowed mother near past an age to bear. They think we are both mad.'

Mad they were. But then, her lady had always been mad for, or with, love. It was a privilege most women of her birth were not allowed, yet Joan grasped it with both hands. She was the descendant of a King, born to all privilege. Why should this one be denied?

Anne swallowed the thought and kept her fingers moving to create even stitches, as her lady liked them.

'But we could not wait,' Joan said, speaking as much to herself as to Anne. 'You know we could not wait.'

'No, of course,' Anne agreed by habit, uncertain

which of her weddings Lady Joan was thinking of. For what her lady wanted could never, never wait.

'The pestilence is all around us. It could fell us at any time. We wanted...'

Ah, yes. She spoke of Edward, then.

This time, the pestilence had struck grown men and small children hardest. Even the King's oldest friend had been taken. The Prince, any of them, might be dead tomorrow.

The reminder stilled her fingers. Since birth, Anne had needed all her strength just to cling to survival.

'Do *you* think we're mad, Anne?' The voice, instead of commanding an answer, was wistful, as if she hoped Anne would answer *no*.

She sounded once again as she had all those years ago. Just for a moment, no longer a woman with royal blood, born to command, but a woman in love, desperate for reassurance that miracles were possible.

Joan had worn the same face then. Blue eyes wide, fair curls about her face, pleading, as if one person were all the difference between Heaven and Earth.

How could she answer now? Joan *was* mad. Playing with the laws of God and men as if she had the right. And suddenly, Anne wished fiercely she could do the same.

Such choices did not exist for a cripple.

'It is not for me to say, my lady.'

Joan rose and gathered Anne's fingers away from her needle, playing with them as she had when they were young. 'But I want you to celebrate with me. With us.'

Ah, yes. That was Joan. Still able to wind everyone she knew into a ball of yarn she could toss at will. So Anne sighed and hugged her, and said she was happy for her and all would be well, succumbing to Joan's charm as everyone did. It was her particular gift, to draw love to herself as the sea drew the river.

'It is settled, then,' Joan said, all smiles again. 'All will be as it must.'

'Of course, my lady.' Words by rote. A response as thoughtless as her lady's watchwords.

But her lady was not finished. 'Have you seen him? The King's ambassador, Sir Nicholas?'

Anne's heart sped at the memory. 'From afar.'

'So he has not seen you.'

She shook her head, grateful he had been spared the sight of her stumbling as she stared after him.

'Good. Then here is what you must do for me.'

Anne put down her needlework and listened.

An honour, of course, the life she lived. Many would envy a position at the court, surrounded by luxury. And yet, some days, it felt more like a dungeon, for she would never be allowed to leave her lady's side.

She knew too much.

Nicholas stood in an alcove on the edge of the Great Room of the largest of the King's four lodges, watching Edward and Joan celebrate as if they were already wed in the eyes of God and his priests.

All evening, men had come up to him, slapping

him on the shoulder as if the battle were over and he had won a great victory.

He had not. Not yet.

A swig of claret did not help him swallow that truth, though Edward and Joan seemed to have no trouble ignoring it. Still, the Pope's message had been private, not his to share. Nothing more than a formality. A few more weeks of inconvenience, then he'd find freedom.

He scanned the room, impatient to be gone. The treaty with France was a year old, but Nicholas had spent little of it in England. King Edward now held the French King's own sons as hostages and Nicholas had been one of those charged with the comings and goings of men and of gold.

Now, instead of meeting the French in battle, King Edward, as chivalrous as Arthur, treated them as honoured guests instead of prisoners of war. He had even brought some of them to this forest hideaway to protect them from the pestilence.

Well, a live hostage was worth gold. A dead one was worth nothing. And Nicholas's own French hostage, securely held in a gaol in London, would be worth something.

One day.

The King had called for dancing and some of the French hostages had joined in, laughing and flirting with Princess Isabella, who was nearly the age of the Prince and unmarried. Strange, that such a wise ruler as Edward had not yet married off his oldest children. Unused assets, too long accustomed to living as they pleased, both of them were strong willed and open to mischief.

Someone bumped into him, hard enough that his wine sloshed from the cup and splashed his last clean tunic. He turned, frowning, ready to call out to the clumsy knave.

Instead, he saw a woman.

Well, he did not see *her* exactly. The first thing he saw, he felt as it brushed over his hand, was her hair. Soft and red and smelling vaguely of spices.

A surge of desire caught him off guard. It had been a long time since he had bedded a woman, or even thought of one.

She had fallen and he swallowed the sharp retort he had planned and held out a hand to help her rise. 'Watch yourself.'

She looked up at him, eyes wide, then quickly looked down. 'Forgive me.'

Humble words. But not a humble tone.

She raised her eyes again and he saw in their depths that she was accustomed to serving the rich. He knew that feeling and wondered who she waited on.

'I am sorry,' she said, in a tone that implied she had used the words many times. 'Usually there is no one here and I can catch a moment of quiet.'

'I spoke too harshly.' Life at court demanded strength and courtesy in a different mix from the work of war and diplomacy.

He grabbed her hand to help her up, ignoring the fire on his palm, thinking she would let go quickly.

She did not.

Her fingers remained in his, not lightly, as if she were attempting seduction, but heavily as if she would fall without his support.

'Can you stand now?' Eager to have his hand returned.

Her eyes met his and did not look away this time. 'If you hand me my stick.'

Too late, he saw it. A crutch, fallen to the floor.

He looked down at her skirt before he could stop himself, then forced his eyes to meet hers again.

Hers had a weary expression, as if he were not the first curious person who had sought a glimpse of her defect. 'It is a feeble foot and not much to look on.'

He did not waste breath to deny where his gaze had fallen. 'Lean against the wall. I'll get your stick.'

She did and he bent over, feeling strangely unbalanced, as if he might topple, too. The movement brought his hand and his cheek too close to her skirt and he caught himself wondering what lay beneath, not the foot she had spoken of, but the more womanly parts…

Abruptly, he stood and handed the smooth, worn stick to her, straight armed, as if she might catch sight of his thoughts if he got too close.

She reached for the staff, tucked it under her arm, then stretched her free hand to brush the stain on his tunic. 'I will have this washed.'

He grabbed her fingers and nearly threw her hand away from his chest. 'No need.' Ashamed, with his next breath, that he had done so. She would think it was because of her leg.

It was not. It was because her fingers lit a fire within him. 'Forgive my lack of chivalry.' He had been too long at war and too little around women.

She laughed then. A laugh devoid of mirth, yet it rolled through her with the deep reverberation of a bell.

A bell calling him not to church, but to something much more earthly.

When her laughter faded, she smiled. 'I am not a woman accustomed to chivalry.'

He studied her, puzzled. She would not have drawn his eye in a room. Hair the colour of fabric ill—dyed, as if it wanted to be red but had not the strength. An unremarkable face except for her eyes. Large, wide set, bold and stark, taking over her face, yet he could not name their colour. Blue? Grey?

'What are you accustomed to?' he asked.

Not a serving woman. She was too well dressed and, despite his first impression, did not have the cowering demeanour of those of that station.

'I am Anne of Stamford, lady-in-waiting to the Countess of Kent.'

The Countess of Kent. Or, as she would soon be known, the Princess of Wales. The woman whose want of discretion had sent him to Avignon and back.

'I am Sir Nicholas Lovayne.' Though she had not shown the courtesy to ask.

'The King's emissary to His Holiness,' she finished. Her eyes, fixed on him. 'I know.'

He shifted his stance, moving a step away. His mission was no secret, but her tone suggested she knew more of his news than the courtiers who had slapped his back in congratulations.

He wondered what the Lady Joan had told her.

'Then you know,' he said, cautiously, 'what a celebration this is.'

She looked out over the room, without the smile he might have expected. 'Not until they are wed in truth. Then, we will celebrate.'

We. As if she and her lady were the same person. So they were close, this maiden and her lady.

Why would Lady Joan choose such a woman as a close companion? If one discounted her lameness, this Anne would not draw a second glance. Perhaps, then, that *was* the reason. Perhaps the Countess wanted someone who would not distract from her own beauty.

If so, she had chosen well.

'Then let us hope we truly celebrate soon,' he said. Celebrate and let him leave for the unencumbered life he wanted.

'That will depend on you, won't it?'

Close indeed, if she had been told so much.

He threw back the last swallow of claret. An unpleasant reminder of the task still before him. A waste of time, to look for things that had been proven to the satisfaction of God's representative on earth long ago. 'It will depend on how quickly the Archbishop can locate a dozen-year-old document.'

'Is that all that must be done?'

He certainly hoped so. 'His Holiness can expect no more. Except to prick the King's ease.'

'And will it be difficult?'

Full of questions. He glanced at the table at the end of the Hall. His answers, no doubt, would go directly to her mistress. 'No.'

'We are all just…' The pause seemed wistful. 'Ready for it to be over.'

'As am I,' he said. He felt like that Greek fellow. Hercules. One labour ended, another began. Surely he had reached his dozen.

They exchanged smiles, as if they were old friends. 'A few weeks only,' he assured her. 'Less, if I can make it so.'

'You sound as eager for the conclusion as I. What awaits you, when all this is over?'

Nothing. And that freedom was the appeal. 'I will head back across the Channel.'

'Another duty for the Prince?'

He shook his head. He was done with duties and obligations. 'Not this time. Rather a duty to myself.' Bald to say it. He looked down at his empty cup. 'And now, I leave you to the peace you sought here.'

'Do not leave on my behalf. The Countess will have missed me by now.' She took a step, steadying herself with her crutch.

'Do you need help?' He waved his hand in her direction. How did one assist a cripple?

There was steel in her smile. 'I do this every day.'

Maybe so, he thought, but as she left, her lips tightened and her brow creased. Every day, every step, then, lived in pain.

We are all waiting... Ah, yes. The Prince and Lady Joan were not the only ones depending on him for a quick resolution. So was her lady-in-waiting, he thought, as he watched her leave, rolling and swaying with her awkward gait.

He wondered why she cared so much.

Anne made her way back to the dais, then waited until Lady Joan could break off and they could speak unheard.

'So?' Beneath the smile, her lady's whisper was urgent. 'What did he say?'

Anne shook her head. 'No suspicions.' She had become sensitive to such things. Shrugs, tones of voice. It compensated for other weaknesses. 'He gives little thought to the task except that it be over. He thinks that the Pope only wanted to create one final obstacle in exchange for his blessing.'

'Yes, of course. That must be it. No other reason.' Her lady breathed again. 'All will be as it must. Now that we know, you must avoid Sir Nicholas.'

She knew that. Knew she should for all kinds of reasons. But her stubborn, sinful ingratitude flared again. The resentment that boiled over when Lady Joan, kind as she was, demanded something in the tone she might use to a command her hound or her horse.

No, she must be grateful. She nodded.

Anne looked across the Hall at him. Tall, straight,

well favoured, with eyes that seemed to pierce the walls.

And able to move—oh, God, to move wherever he liked. Back to France for no good reason, as if it were as easy as walking into a room.

She had learned to stifle her envy as she watched women dance on their toes, watched men stride without stopping. But when this stranger took her hand, it was not envy she felt.

It was something worse. Attraction.

She turned away. Maybe it was not this man, maybe it was all that surrounded her. The wedding, the minute-by-minute need that Joan and her Edward felt, as if each was the other's air…

That would never be hers, Anne knew, so she had never let herself want it. Never allowed her eyes to fall on a man and think of him that way. If she were so fortunate as to wed, it would be because some man had taken pity on her and agreed to carry the burden of her in exchange for beautiful stitching and a steady head. And if he did, she would, of course, have no choice but to be abjectly grateful.

Her eyes sought him out again. No, she needed no encouragement to avoid Sir Nicholas Lovayne. She wanted no reminders of things that would never be hers.

Chapter Three

The next day, before dawn, Nicholas was mounted and recalculating the miles between the New Forest and Canterbury. His squire, Eustace, had arrived late in the day with the recovered horse. All was packed and ready, the steed beneath him as impatient as he.

Light seeped through the trees.

Prince Edward did not come.

Instead, he sent a page with the news. The pestilence, that murderous giant, still lumbered in the land. The King forbade the journey, it seemed, until some other hapless soul could travel the route and return to pronounce it safe for his son and heir to traverse.

Biting his tongue, Nicholas swung off the horse and left it for the squire to stable. Strange, the things men feared. Neither Edward the father nor the son had hesitated to face death on the field of battle, but the King had turned timid when he lost the last friend of his youth to The Death. Now, the monarch cowered in a forest, as if death could not find his family here.

Nicholas would not run from death.

It would come for him, as it came for all men. He had survived the war with the French, but there would be other wars to come. In Italy, or even the Holy Land.

Deprived of his journey, Nicholas snapped at all around him like a hungry dog deprived of his bone. Restless, he left the hunting lodge, too small to comfortably hold even a temporary court, to prowl the grounds. He pulled three cloth balls from his pouch, juggling them to keep his hands busy, recalculating the miles to Canterbury and back.

Eyes on his hands, mind on his task, he nearly tripped over Anne sitting on a small bench that caught the morning sun.

Her needlework fell to the ground. She bent over, but he was faster, snatching it from the dirt more quickly than she could.

Dusting her work off, he handed it back to her. 'It seems that fetching your dropped items has become a habit of mine.'

After the words had left his tongue, he realised how ill chosen they were.

She took it without touching his fingers. No smile sweetened her sharp expression. 'My thanks.' Words without feeling.

Now that the embroidery filled her hands again, her fingers flew in a way her feet never would and she bent to her work, ignoring him. A beautiful piece, though he was no judge of such things. Silver on black. Then, he recognised it. The Prince had used such a badge.

He slipped his juggling balls into his pouch. 'You prepare for their wedding.' She did not look up from her stitches.

'Do not tell the Prince. Lady Joan plans a gift to celebrate the wedding.'

'I can be discreet,' though he realised he had not been so with her last night.

'I'm glad of it,' she said, still bowed over her needle. 'All will be as it must.'

Strange words. 'And how must it be?'

Laughter escaped again. So unexpected. As if all the beauty and ease denied her body was lodged in her throat. 'It must be as God, or my lady, wishes.'

His life, captured in the words. All must be as the Prince, and the King, wanted. Horses to Calais. Wine across the Seine. Documents to Avignon. Always leave a way out. Always have an alternate route.

He would have no more of the wishes of others.

'And do God's wishes align with those of the Countess?'

A smile teased her lips. 'Thanks to the Pope and to Sir Nicholas Lovayne, yes.'

He could not help but smile. Yes, he was ready to be free of such demands, but as long as they were his, he would fulfil each one. Including this last. 'So is there to be a magnificent wedding ceremony in Canterbury?'

Anne shook her head and looked back at her needlework. 'She wishes it to be done quickly.'

'No pomp? No circumstance?' No huge celebration of all his work? 'She is of royal blood and marrying the future King. There has been no such wedding since…' When? Before he was born.

She looked at him sharply. 'Appropriate to their station, yes, but she is wedding the man she wants.'

'She wants?' A much more urgent and earthy word than *loves* or even *needs*. One that conveyed a stiff staff and a welcoming hole. One uncomfortably like what he was feeling for the woman before him. 'I persuaded the Pope to bend the laws of God for what she *wants?*'

Words he should not have said. Her wide eyes told him so.

'You were sent,' she said, as if teaching a child, 'because you could accomplish the task. You should feel humbly grateful for the trust placed in you.'

'Grateful?' No, that was not what he felt. Instead, it was that most serious of the seven deadly sins: pride. 'I only hope it is worth the cost.'

'To you?'

A sharp tongue, this one. Sharp enough to puncture his moment of desire for her. Despite her lectures, she seemed no more humbly grateful than he.

He cleared his throat and collected his wits. 'To me it is, yes.' Well worth it. Now, he would be free. 'I meant worth the cost to them.' The cost of the chapels alone was more than Nicholas would see in his lifetime.

Her needle paused, for the first time, and she gazed beyond him, as if he had disappeared. 'To be able to look at someone that way…?'

'As if they cannot wait until darkness?' His words

were more than reckless, but, in just weeks, he would no longer be the Prince's thrall.

She shook her head. 'It is more than lust.'

That, he could not argue. It was madness. 'The Prince is…' Every word he tried sounded like an insult. The Prince acted like a man bewitched. His own father had looked so, when he married his second wife. Bewitched and blind to the truth of her.

Anne gazed up at him, as if she understood the meaning he could not find words for. 'Blissful. He is blissful. She is the same.'

He shook his head. Bliss would not last. His father's had not. 'I have never seen him so before. But then, he has never been wed.'

Now she looked at him, her eyes—what colour would he name them?—unwavering on his. 'And she has? Is that your meaning?'

As if she knew thoughts he easily hid from others.

Did the woman speak so bluntly to the Countess? If so, she would not be a comfortable companion. 'Have you recently come to her service?' If so, perhaps she would not be there long.

'No. I have been with her for a long time.'

Perhaps through all the marriages, official and otherwise. Perhaps she could save him a trip to Canterbury. 'Were you there when she and Thomas Holland wed?'

She pricked her finger and popped it in her mouth. His gaze lingered on her lips longer than it should have. He was thinking of *wants,* of *needs*…

'You are right,' she said, finally, glancing down at

the Prince's badge, fallen again to the earth. 'I seem to be ever dropping things at your feet. Could you hand it to me again?'

For a moment, he could not look away from her lips. Thin, yes, but finely drawn, an apology from the Creator for what he had done to her leg.

Nicholas forced his eyes away and picked up the needlework again, glad of the excuse to break his gaze, struggling to remember his thoughts.

'Are you a juggler, Sir Nicholas?'

He thought she had not noticed. 'Only to amuse myself.' He remembered now, as he returned her stitchery to her, his question. Had she wanted him to forget? 'Her marriage to Holland. Were you there?'

'Yes, of course. It was a quiet affair.'

'I meant the first time.'

She looked away. 'The first time? Her marriage to Salisbury, you mean?'

'No. Her first marriage to Holland. The secret one.'

She pursed the thin lips. 'I was but four. They did not have a babbling babe present.'

He thought of her at four and smiled.

She did not. 'Now, as you have reminded me, I have duties to perform in the here and now.' She put the needlework in a pouch and reached for her walking stick.

'Let me…' He reached to help her, still not knowing why, again resenting her for his discomfort.

She turned a frigid gaze on him. 'I have lived twenty-five years without your help. I do not need it now.'

He gritted his teeth to hold back sharp words. 'Then I shall not offer it again.'

He watched her hobble away, anger mixing with guilt for thinking ill of her when he should be filled with pity.

Yet pity was the last thing he felt. She wore her limp as proudly as a knight might wore his scars earned by prowess in war.

No, he was feeling something else even more surprising.

Want.

He shook his head, trying to clear his mind. He had been too long without a woman. On his trip to Canterbury, he'd make a detour to Grape Lane and find a woman with fair hair and lush lips and blue eyes who did not hurl prickly insults at him.

Strange, he puzzled again, watching her stumble back to the lodge, for Lady Joan to keep such a woman with her, and not only because of her tart tongue. Typically, such persons were shunned, or discreetly kept out of sight. This woman, on the other hand, was ever close to her lady. And while she could not agilely leap to perform tasks, she seemed to be in charge of others who did.

Well, he was not here to wonder about a lady-in-waiting. He was here to make sure the Prince could wed his lady love.

After that, he'd be gone.

'Come, Anne,' Lady Joan said, patting the bench beside her as Anne returned to her chambers. 'Where have you been? We must speak of all that is to be done before the wedding.'

Anne hobbled over to the bench and sank onto it, more tired than usual. Her first thought was to tell her lady that Nicholas had asked dangerous questions.

Her second thought was to keep that secret to herself.

But her lady, speaking of the wedding, did not question further, so Anne pulled out her needle and thread and settled in to listen.

Her lady demanded all her attention and more. She was as jumpy as a cat, Anne thought, prowling the chamber, speaking of one idea, then another, her fabled calm shattered.

Lady Joan was unaccustomed to being without a man. When Thomas Holland had been gone to war, well, that was one thing. But he died late in December, in Normandy, she by his side. It had been a blur, those next weeks. Packing, moving back across the Channel. Anne had expected peace and mourning when they returned.

But her lady was not a woman who could live for long without a husband. How many weeks had it been after they returned before she was looking for her next companion? Barely enough to mourn the man. And Joan was not only the most beautiful woman in England, she was also the most wealthy. She had her pick of men, clustered, pleading their cases.

But she had waited for the best catch of them all. And a man she had known in the nursery.

Anne had no opinion about Edward of Woodstock.

She couldn't afford to. Some tongues had wagged. The lusty widow. But if it had been Anne, the Prince would not have stirred her lust.

Unbidden, she thought of Nicholas. He of the strong brows and the rugged nose and the lips that...

She shook her head. The man's lips were no longer of any interest to her unless they were speaking of something of interest to her lady.

'We must craft the celebration carefully,' the Countess was saying. 'It must not be so gay that it dishonours those taken by the pestilence, yet it must be grand and appropriate to a future King and Queen.' A perplexed pout quivered on her lips. 'And yet, it is a ceremony for two who are already married.'

'Not in the eyes of the Pope.' Anne swallowed, wishing she could recall the words. She knew better than to speak so bluntly to her lady. Sparring with Sir Nicholas had made her tongue tart.

Lady Joan blinked, as if her pet monkey had suddenly nipped her. 'The Pope will get his chapels. All will be as it must.'

'If Sir Nicholas obtains the proper blessing from the Archbishop.'

Now, the Countess turned her full gaze on her. 'You assured me there was nothing to fear. Have you spoken to him again? Has something changed?'

Yes. He was asking questions, the very questions neither she, nor her lady, wanted to answer. But to say so would be to admit she had whiled away a few minutes in the sunshine with a handsome knight who actually looked at *her*. To admit that instead of avoiding him, she had spoken to him of *wants*...

She cleared her throat and shook her head, looking at her stitches instead of at her lady. 'I only mean that if he is looking into the past, he might become curious. He might ask more questions.'

Reassured, the Countess waved her hand. 'He will find little.'

That, of course, was what she was afraid of. And what would Nicholas Lovayne do then? No doubt he would be loyal to his Prince, just as she was to her lady.

'I know!' The Lady Joan stopped her pacing. 'After the wedding, we'll have a celebration. A tournament before all the people to prove that we have triumphed over the death that haunts our land.'

Anne smoothed her fingers over the silver stitches, holding back a pointed reply. Only Jesus Christ triumphed over death.

But her lady was speaking of dresses and colours...

'Shall he come to the wedding?'

'Who?' Her lady returned to the bench and placed cool fingers on Anne's forehead. 'Are you ill? You are not like yourself today.'

No, she was not. She was still dizzy with confusion. 'I meant Sir Nicholas. Since he helped to make it possible.'

A shrug. 'I suppose so.'

'Then how am I to avoid him? Until he leaves for

Canterbury, I cannot refuse to speak to him without creating questions.'

The smile, always the smile that disguised the workings of her lady's mind. Anne tried to compose her face so, but she was not good at lies.

'No, no. I see. You are right. He has done us a great service.' She patted Anne's hand. 'Stay close to him. Treat him as a close friend.'

She had wanted only forgiveness for the sin already committed, not an obligation to seek him out again. 'I am not a woman to capture a man's attentions.'

The look of pity on Lady Joan's face made her wince. No. Her lady had not thought so either. 'I only meant you should keep him amused. Diverted. Men without war must be kept busy.'

'Perhaps that would be better left to someone who could dance with him.' The thought of deliberately getting close to Nicholas Lovayne unsettled her. As if she might, like the moth, singe her wings on the flame.

'A woman need not dance with a man to keep him entertained.'

Anne knew that as well as anyone. She knew enough how to distract people so they would not notice…other things. She made the final stitch on the Prince's badge, glad to lay it aside. Black and silver were dreary colours. 'This one is finished, my lady.'

'Good. Now, show me how the *aumônière* is coming. Will it be ready next week?'

Anne put aside the Prince's badge to show her lady

the needlework that would become an alms purse. Because her feet did not work, her fingers worked even harder. How many pouches had she created in her time? Ten? Twenty? Fifty? Each one given away for a man to give to his lady, or for a lady to entice her man.

This one showed two lovers, standing side by side in a garden, the lady fair and smiling.

'Your stitching is as expert as the guild's work, Anne. This looks just like Edward and me.'

'Thank you, my lady.'

And because she pleased the Lady Joan, Anne did not have to beg for alms from men and women with purses such as these.

'I know! Make one of these for Sir Nicholas to give to his lady as a thank you from me. Find out who she is. That will keep his thoughts away from other things.'

His lady. Of course he must have one. 'But what if it doesn't?' Anne knew enough of him to know he was not a stupid man. 'What if he asks of things he must not know?'

Lady Joan paused, staring at Anne as if she had not understood the question. 'Why, then, you will lie,' she said, as if she had said Anne might sup on beef stew.

Chapter Four

You will lie.

Could she? When she opened her mouth, would the words come out?

She would, because she must.

Because her whole life was a lie.

She reminded herself of that, after the evening meal, when she looked for Nicholas in the Hall. Her lady had asked that she befriend him and befriend him she would, ignoring the fact that the idea appealed to her for reasons her lady must not know.

As before, she saw him standing alone at the edge of the Hall, looking out over the dancers. She joined him, relieved he had not moved in the time it took for her to hobble to his side. He could easily escape her and she could not chase him around the Hall.

'I hope you do not mind my company,' she said, as she sank onto the bench and leaned against the stone wall. Her leg ached and she wished she could rub it.

'I wonder why you seek mine,' he said, in a sour tone. 'I seem to do nothing but insult you.'

She felt heat in her cheeks. 'Forgive me. I must be ever pleasant and positive with the Countess.' She pulled her needlework out from its pouch and fumbled with the needle and thread. 'Sometimes, I...' She bit her tongue.

'Tire of it?'

'Do you not? Are there not times you want to say something the Prince would not wish to hear?'

He smiled, sheepishly.

So that had happened. Recently. 'I can see that you have.' She wondered what impolitic thing he had wanted to say. And whether it had been about her lady.

'I'll keep your secret,' he said, the smile warmer now, 'if you'll keep mine.'

She had to return his grin and, for a moment, she felt as if they were partners instead of adversaries.

'You have my promise,' she said.

Relationships, promises, loyalties. In the end, that was all a King had. That was what allowed him to rule. That was what kept the world from falling utterly to dust and what kept Anne from starving alone.

Nicholas was loyal to Edward. He would find what Edward wanted him to find.

All would be as it must.

As she stitched, the noise of the after-supper entertainment rose. Singing, dancing, the tumbling and juggling echoed around the hall.

Old Robert the Fool rolled across the floor in a somersault, then jumped to his feet in front of them, tossing and catching five painted wooden balls. 'And who is this new arrival come before us?'

'A juggler like yourself,' she answered, putting down the alms purse. 'Sir Nicholas Lovayne.'

He turned to her with a frown.

She ignored him.

'Ah,' Old Robert said, both tongue and hands still moving, 'this is the miracle worker I've heard of. The one who can make Eve into the Virgin Mary.'

Shamed, Anne flushed, silent. Fools had licence others did not, but it was a blatant reference to her lady. And not a flattering one. She hoped Joan would never hear of it.

'Look lively, Sir Miracle Worker.' The fool tossed a ball to Nicholas.

Astonished, she watched him catch it and throw it back and suddenly, they were juggling the five between them and Nicholas was smiling again.

When, finally, he missed a catch, he picked up the fallen ball and tossed it to Old Robert with ease. 'I'm not your match, Fool.'

'Ah, it depends on the game, doesn't it?' He winked at them and moved on.

She cleared her throat. 'He has been with the King for many years. He assumes privileges.'

He shrugged. 'A fool's words are not worth repeating.'

Able to breathe again, she turned back to her stitching, watching Nicholas out of the corner of her eye.

Loyal to the Prince, he would spread no tales. And yet he sat alone while Edward the father and Edward the son cast bets on the throw of the die with other knights and nobles.

She met his eyes and nodded toward the laughing group in the corner. 'You do not join them?'

He turned to follow her glance. 'Life itself seems a game of chance. I do not actively seek uncertainty.'

'You have spent years at war. There is no certainty there.'

'More than you would think. We are certain to ride long days, certain to be hungry, certain to fight. I control all the things I can, but in the end, I am certain to either live or die.'

'As God wills.'

'Or the King. Or your lady.'

She must have stared for a moment, shocked at his words. Blasphemy, no doubt, but they reflected her own life, lived at the mercy of someone else.

'Yet you return to France.' She must keep him speaking of himself so he would not think of questioning her. 'Why?'

A wisp of longing washed over his face. 'To return to war.'

'But the war is over.' A truce was signed. French hostages crowded the court.

'Is it?' He looked down at her, brow raised, as if she were no wiser than a child, then shrugged. 'There will be another. Somewhere.'

'And you care not where you fight? Or why?'

'Men fight for only one reason. To stay alive.'

'You don't want a home?' *A wife?* 'Here in England?'

He shook his head. 'I would rather keep moving.'

Envy tasted bitter. 'Will you not wed?'

'Of course.' His voice, hearty, but bitter. 'To a wealthy widow.'

'Ah.' She swallowed, ashamed of the direction of her thoughts. Of course he would marry. He was tall and strong. His legs, long and straight, stretched out before him, a deliberate insult to her own. The old King, Longshanks, must have had limbs such as these. 'Will she be here soon?'

'She? Who?'

'Your…' She had a moment's jealousy of the woman who would lie in his arms. 'The widow.' Someone for whom she could stitch an alms purse.

He shook his head, eyes downcast. 'There is no widow. But that's what every poor knight wants, is it not?'

'I'm sure I don't know what a poor knight wants.' She kept her eyes on her work, ashamed that she had asked. There would be no one for her. Ever. And asking embarrassing questions of a handsome knight would change nothing.

'I answered rudely. Your question was an honest one. What this poor knight wants is the ransom for his French hostage.'

'So you've a prisoner?' Keep the talk of him. Do not let him ask questions about her or her lady.

He nodded. 'The reward for all my months of fighting.'

She looked out over the Hall where some of the French hostages were exchanging lingering glances with the ladies. 'Is he here?'

'He's safely locked up in London, dining at my expense.'

'But you'll be paid for that, with the ransom.'

'The French have been slow with ransom payments.'

She nodded. That much she knew. 'And while we wait for French *livres,* the hostages entertain themselves with food and wine and gambling.'

'That we must pay for. I sometimes wonder whether it would be cheaper for the French to pay the ransom than to keep paying their expenses here.'

Something she had never considered. He was a man accustomed to thinking of the cost of things. Her lady never did, even after the bill was presented. 'Yet you are a fortunate man,' she said. 'You have a hostage. He will bring you gold.'

'Forgive my ingratitude.' He looked abashed and she was sorry. 'I must seem rude. I'm just ready to be quit of him and back to France.'

'No! I like that you do not...hold your tongue.' So few were so blunt. Fewer still would speak of movement without a downward glance at her poor leg. 'I envy you your journey. I would love to see...so much.'

'Have you not been out of England?'

'Yes, of course. The Lady Joan was in France when her husband, Lord Holland, died.' They had gone when her lady willed and returned when her lady willed. And all the while, unexplored horizons beckoned.

He looked at her, his glance too perceptive. 'And when next she returns, you will, too.'

'They speak of Aquitaine. A kingdom of his own for the Prince.'

He grunted and took a sip of claret.

Again, she waited in vain for him to speak. Finally, she tried again. 'You do not approve?'

He looked at her, his expression more shock than sneer. 'My opinion makes no difference.'

A feeling she well knew. 'But you have been there.'

He nodded.

'And would you return?' He, a man who had travelled across France. He would know whether it was a place she would like.

'There is no need. We subdued it.'

So clear that this man knew no life but war. 'I mean, should we—I mean, should the Prince and my lady go, will it be a pleasant place to live?'

'A flat land with rivers. Hard to defend. The bridges need to be rebuilt.'

No mention of whether the rivers were wide and blue or narrow and rushing. No word of green leaves or yellow flowers or whether the sun was warm or the wine sweeter near its own soil. 'Can you speak of nothing but horses and supplies and fighting?'

His eyes cleared of memory and recognised her once more. 'That's why I was there.'

There with eyes focused not on the land, but on how they must move over it and what they must do to subdue it. 'But I will not be there for war.'

'The Prince will.'

'But his wife will not. I hope there will be time to see other things.'

Quiet, but intent, he studied her. 'What things? What things would you choose to see?'

She looked away, abashed by the perception of the question. If she were as tall and strong as he and free to choose her life, she would walk from here to Compostela to see the shrine of St James and from there to Rome, where the ancient stones of the Romans still stood. And beyond that lay Castile or Jerusalem or even Alexandria...

But those were dreams for someone else, not for a lame girl.

'I go where my lady chooses.' And was fortunate to do so. Fool. She had let the man turn questions on her and then been foolish enough to answer them.

She bowed her head over her needlework, grateful that the music and chatter had masked their words. She must turn the talk back to him before she said something else to regret. Dancers gathered before them on the floor as the minstrels lifted pipes and bows.

Turning back to Nicholas, she gave him her broadest smile. 'Do you dance?'

Nicholas looked at Anne, uncertain what to say. Anything he said would be an insult to a woman who would never skip gaily through a circle dance.

'There was little dancing in the midst of battle.' It was the truth.

She looked up from her stitching and smiled, as if she realised the foolishness of the question. 'Was there no respite from the fighting?'

'The King made time for hawking.' Which meant Nicholas had arranged for the care and feeding of the King's favourite birds as well as of men.

'Ah.' She had a way of looking from her stitching to his face and back in a natural rhythm. 'I have ridden after the falcons. Once. Or twice.'

She could ride, then. He had wondered.

His surprise must have shown plain on his face, for she answered it. 'The falconer does most of the work.'

'I did not think—'

'I know what you thought.' Her needle paused.

He, a man who cloaked his feelings from royalty, had allowed this woman to see his very thoughts. Dangerous.

Then, as if she had seen his dismay, she touched his hand with fingers straight and slender, some mad form of amends for her leg.

'Forgive me,' she said. 'Sometimes I try to ignore that which is perfectly obvious. You did nothing wrong.'

He wondered whether she had confessed so much to others. 'You take your…situation…with remarkable calm.'

'I have no choice. What else can I do?'

No choice. He shuddered. He had lived his life making sure that there were always choices, options, other paths to follow.

'You could rail against your fate and insist on special treatment.' He knew able-bodied warriors more peevish with less reason.

'That would change nothing.'

He had no answer to that and the silence between them grew until, as the music ended, he realised her fingers still rested on the back of his hand. She saw them at the same moment and pulled them away, as if from a fire.

'Will you join tomorrow's hunt?' Thoughtless words to cover the awkward moment. It was a deer hunt, demanding in a way that hawking was not.

And he was looking forward to it. He would ride as long and hard and fast as the running stag they chased. He would outride all the frustration of being stuck here because the King was overcautious.

Her fingers were busy with her needle again, the rhythm restored. 'They have little patience with me on the hunt.'

'Women ride.' Some of them. 'And there is no shame in lagging behind.'

'Not as far behind as I do.'

Was her smile as wistful as he imagined? He supposed it would be a kind of death, to be left behind, trapped, while the rest of the court galloped off on a sunny summer day.

'Come,' he said, abruptly. He had seen slaughter enough in France. No need to witness the death of every deer. 'I'll ride beside you.'

Her needle shook, but her stitches did not pause. 'Pity for the cripple?'

He grabbed her wrist, stopping her needle and forcing her to look at him. 'No.'

She met his eyes, questioning, and he wondered what she saw there. In truth, he did not know why he had offered and more words would only make it worse.

Finally, she smiled, a slow, lovely thing. 'I would like that.'

'Tomorrow, then.' He stood abruptly and with a curt bow escaped.

As quickly as that, he had committed himself to spend time with a woman who would do nothing but drag him down.

Chapter Five

The next morning, regretting his impulse of the previous day, Nicholas joined the rest as they gathered outside the lodge, in preparation for the hunt.

He hoped that a page would appear, telling him Anne had changed her mind, leaving him free to ride off his restlessness.

Yet there she was, already on horseback, waiting for him at the edge of the chaos surrounding the assembly. Dogs who would track the deer sniffed the air, wondering which scent they would follow. Dogs ready to chase the deer chased their tails instead, held back by their handlers until the quarry was sighted. In the suit of green he favoured for the hunt, the King conferred with his huntsman, considering their plan.

And Anne, seated atop a bay courser, looked out over the scene as if to memorise it.

If he asked her outright whether she could manage a day on horseback, would she back down? Without opening his mouth, he knew the answer. Still, he might give her the opportunity…

'He uses the dogs,' Nicholas said, glancing at the King while laying a comforting palm on the neck of Anne's horse. Dogs meant a longer hunt. Gruelling and gruesome. He looked up at Anne, hoping for a reprieve.

She nodded. 'They've located a hart of ten.' A stag with ten points on his antlers. 'He'll be a worthy opponent.'

No wonder the King was smiling.

'It will be a long day, then.' They would be hunting *par force,* as the King preferred, chasing the beast into exhaustion. The work had begun the day before for the huntsman and continued with a discussion over a morning meal that Nicholas had decided to miss.

Now, they had to set the dogs along the path and have the scent hound find the beast again. When they did, the hounds would give chase. Finally, it might be hours later, when the beast was at bay, the King would get the honour of making the kill and unmaking the animal, cutting it carefully to pieces and giving the dogs their taste as a reward. All this could keep them on horseback until near dark.

'So my lady hopes.' She nodded toward the Prince and his intended, mounted and waiting side by side. Lady Joan raised a hand and waved to Anne. 'Without war, the men grow restless.' She looked down at him. 'Don't you?'

She said it as if she knew how eager he was to join the chase.

'Yes.' The word sounded churlish.

'Then it is good that we hunt today.' She spoke with a smile and without any indication that she was ready to get off her horse.

He sighed and mounted the hunting horse he had borrowed from the King's stable. The day might be longer than even he expected.

King Edward gave the signal and they moved out, slowly at first, as the huntsman and the handlers went ahead to confirm the scent and put the chasers in position.

The New Forest was the King's private deer park. Here, the animals could roam and breed unhindered by any but royalty. Dappled sunlight came and went through the lush green canopy of leaves, ruffled by a breeze perfect for bringing the scent of the deer to the eager dogs.

He glanced at the woman beside him. Slow on her feet, she was less awkward on the horse. The beast's four legs carried her where her three could not. It was not so much the hunt she enjoyed, he decided. It was the freedom to run where her poor body could not take her.

'If we do not keep up,' he began, 'will you mind missing the kill?'

'I like being on the horse and in the fresh air. I do not like seeing…' she faced him and there was truth in her eyes '…harm come to weaker creatures.'

Weaker creatures. As she was. A woman, even a

man with her lameness might be savaged for such a flaw. He had seen it. Blind men armed with sticks told there was a pig for them to feast on if they could kill it. But there was no pig. There was only another man, as blind as the first, so the two ended up beating each other for the amusement of the sighted.

Suddenly, he was angry on her behalf for all the ignorant people who had, or would ever, hurt her. A strange and unwelcome thought.

He had lived as he wanted for so long, detached, thinking only of how to keep men and horses moving or how to get a pope to bless Prince Edward's match. Suddenly, he had heard the woman beside him, recognised her pain, and cared. An unfamiliar and uncomfortable feeling.

Feeling led to disappointment. To mourning a mother who was gone and a new mother who did not care.

And this woman needed no sympathy from him. She was well taken care of now and, once her lady married the Prince, she'd have a life most would envy. Few cripples, even a dwarf who served as a jester, could hope for as much.

He glanced to his side to see how she fared on the horse. Pain and joy mixed uneasily on her face. Tight lips a testament to her struggle not to fall off the courser's back, yet eyes that looked out on the day so eagerly that a smile broke the lock that pain held on her mouth.

Well for the moment, yet she could not ride the

day long this way and it would be impossible for her to keep up once the chase began.

A horn sounded. The deer had been found. The men hurried their horses ahead, hooves trampling the grass, leaving the women to come as they pleased, arriving, perhaps, to celebrate the successful kill.

Nicholas's horse started to trot, as eager as his rider to join the chase. He pulled the reins, holding back the animal, and himself. He could not race off and leave her here, struggling to keep her seat.

Where was Lady Joan? When she dropped back, he could leave Anne with her. But as the Prince dashed ahead, Joan urged her horse to follow.

He looked over at Anne. 'She rides with him?'

She nodded. 'They do not leave each other's sight unless they must.'

The King's daughter Isabella and a few of her ladies trotted ahead, far enough behind the men that they would not have to breathe their dust and far enough ahead of him that he knew Anne could not keep up.

He was trapped.

He had a fleeting hope that he could take her to the lodge and then race back, fast enough to catch the rest in time for the kill.

One glance at the slump of her shoulders ended that thought.

He had spent years and miles on a horse. His thighs were practised at gripping his mount, his feet at steering the horse with a touch.

But her right foot could not stay in the stirrup.

Every shift by her mount threatened to land her in the dirt. Riding for hours would be a constant struggle. Chasing the stag impossible.

And yet, she had tried.

The rest of the riders disappeared, the sound of pounding hooves fading until all he could hear was the rustle of leaves.

He sighed. 'Come.' He nodded at a fallen tree. 'Let's rest.'

'There is no need.' Her stubborn words shook.

He ignored them.

He dismounted and came to help her. She had already been in the saddle when he saw her this morning and he had never thought to wonder how she'd managed it. Could she mount and dismount alone?

He reached for her and she swung her lame, right leg over the saddle and slid down into his arms.

Close. Too close. Her breasts pressed his chest, her breath brushed his cheek, and he caught a scent like the orange fruit from Spain he had tasted, at once sweet and tart.

Her cheek coloured and she seemed to hold her breath.

So did he.

And finally, he did what he had wanted to do ever since she had first bumped against him in the Hall.

He tilted her chin, lifted her lips to his and kissed her.

His first thought—could he even call it that?—was that her lips were softer and warmer than he had expected. His second was that they moved hungrily over his, saying things no other part of her body dared.

And he knew, without knowing how, that no one had ever kissed her before.

Their lips parted slowly. Reluctantly. He let her go and she turned away, reaching for the stick tied to her saddle.

And he waited for a shy maidenly protest. Or a sly, womanly smile, promising hidden delights.

Neither came.

No word. No blush. No smile. No protest. She leaned on her stick and took a step toward the fallen tree as if nothing had happened. As if the kiss were nothing. As if he were nothing.

He gritted his teeth, fighting the unfamiliar feeling roiling his blood. Not rage. Not even lust, though that had stirred, naturally.

No. It was something much less familiar. Possession. Protection. A mad desire to grab her and claim her and call her his.

And she seemed to notice nothing at all.

Anne turned her back on him, afraid to meet his eyes, and took another step.

A blur, all of it. It should not, could not, have happened. Yet she had kissed him. And wanted, oh, so much more.

Why had she come at all? Distract him, her lady had said, not lead him into temptation, though she would not have put it past Lady Joan to ask. But she did not because they both knew it was as impossible as asking Anne to run.

I am not a woman to capture a man's attentions.

And yet, he had kissed her. Deliberately.

And she turned away because if she had not, she might have kissed him again and never stopped.

But his lips, ah, lips not full, but precisely sculpted, seemed to bring her very skin to life. All the strength she had amassed to fight the pain was useless against the pleasure that bloomed from the very whisper of his lips.

Now she must act as if nothing had happened, so she could pretend it had not.

She sank down on to the fallen tree with a sigh of relief.

'You must be tired,' he said, his words quick and meaningless.

And she, who never admitted weakness, nodded, with a weak smile.

'Anne. Look at me.'

She wanted to pretend it had not happened. He would not.

So she lifted her chin and met his eyes, daring him to acknowledge it. 'I forgive you.' Dismissive words. As if she had been affronted, instead of moved.

'I did not ask to be forgiven.'

Only his gaze touched her now, but that was enough. The heat in his eyes reignited the desire she would not, must not feel.

'What do you want, then?' Unable to hold her voice steady. 'To take me out of pity?'

'Pity?' Was that anger in his voice? 'Is that what you think?'

What she thought was to push him so far away that he could not recognise her weakness. 'What I think,' she began, 'is that you thought to steal a kiss, or more, from a vulnerable maiden.'

That would explain it. She should have realised there could be no other reason. He must have thought her easy prey for his lust.

'You are wrong.'

She wanted to be. Oh, she wanted to be.

'Why else would you have lured me here? You knew I could not keep up with the chase. You knew we would fall behind and be alone.' All things she had known before she even mounted.

'Have you met so much unkindness in your life?'

Startled at first. Then, ashamed. She shook her head. 'No. My lady has been all that is kind when I cannot do...what others can.'

'I cannot dance well enough to take the floor before the King. It makes me no lesser man.'

Her eyes widened at his words. Could any man, any person, look at her and not see her as a lesser being?

Yet she saw in his eyes things she had never seen in another man's. Desire, yes, that was remarkable enough. Coupled with anger and a touch of... admiration. Not the pity or disgust she so frequently encountered.

More often though, once they knew who and what she was, they tried not to see her at all. They simply let their eyes slide over her without stopping, as if she were a stone or a tree. Lonely sometimes, yes. But being invisible could be a benefit, as well.

'I am sorry,' she began, 'to attack you when you were only being…kind.' What other word to use?

Something in his gaze shifted. A decision reached. 'Your first notion was the right one. It did not happen. Now, we will sit and speak of unimportant things until you are rested enough to return.'

She did not want to speak with him at all, but she must do as her lady asked and stay close to him, even at the risk of—

No. She straightened her back. There was no risk. She had lived her whole life without a man. That would not change because a passing warrior stole a kiss.

Nicholas settled himself at the other end of the log and sat in silence, relieved when she did not speak, as he struggled to put ground and sky back in their accustomed places.

Fool that he was, he had kissed her. And when he did, the world turned upside down, exposing the weakness he thought safely buried. The same weakness that had blinded his father to the truth about the woman he married.

Yet she thought he wanted only to dally with her and then cast her aside. He should have let her think so. Would that he were so unmoved.

This woman had a way of flinging him from kindness to anger to desire and back before he could understand what had happened. But, it was clear, she wanted an entanglement no more than he did.

Why?

At the other end of the log, she sat, back straight, studying the shaded shelter as if she might be forced to describe it later. Deprived of her accustomed needle, she tapped her restless fingers together without looking at them. He wondered whether she even knew she did so.

What was she thinking now?

He was a man of action, yet he had learned that understanding another man's reasons and impulses was the key to gaining his co-operation. The man who sold wine strictly for money could be persuaded to sell for the right price. The man who was more concerned about his castle's protection might be persuaded to trade in exchange for his loyalty.

He had learned to read such men.

But women? Well, they were not such a mystery. At least, the few he had known were not.

'You have not been around many women.'

Could the woman see his thoughts? 'A fighting man has little time for women.' And that was the way he liked it. Deceivers, all. Willing to say, or do, anything to bejape a man into marriage. Except, it seemed, for this one.

'And I not around many men.'

As close to an apology as this woman would ever come, he guessed.

'We will start again,' he said. 'Not as man or woman,

perhaps.' She wanted that no more than he, he was relieved to realise.

'Men do not usually see a woman when they look at me.'

There was no sorrow in her statement and, again, anger stirred on her behalf. 'Do you not want what other women want?'

'Marriage?' She glanced down at her lap and then back at him, her raised brow and half smile as full as much of pain as pleasure. 'I had judged you a wiser man.'

'Wise enough.' *Except when it comes to you.* Marriage, he guessed, would elude her and his question had only reminded her of that fact.

But of course she wanted it. All women did.

He knew not how to treat this woman or what to say. Her answer to a simple question made him as awkward and unsteady with his words as she was on her feet. Yet she *was* a woman. No reason to believe her any different from the rest. He should have been wary. Instead, he had been lulled.

Anne glanced at Nicholas, who was shaking his head as if he were trying to understand one of the Cornish speakers. Once again, it seemed, she had made him uneasy. It had not been deliberate, but better he be curious about her than about Lady Joan.

Better she turn the questions back at him than let him question her.

'Besides,' she began, 'for every woman who wants

to wed, there must be a man. Few men choose as you have.'

She let the statement dangle, hoping he would offer more of his reasons. Had a woman wronged him? Did he mourn a lost wife? Perhaps he had taken a vow.

'Few men have seen women's full deceit as I have.'

Words harsh as a blow. She must have gasped.

She parted her lips to argue. *I am not like that. I am not like those others you have known.*

But, of course, she was. And to protest would only make the lie grow fat.

He rose and held out his hand. 'If you are rested, we can return.'

She took his hand, needing his help to rise, but let go as quickly as she could, dreading the moment when he would have to help her on to the horse's back.

It was always an awkward thing, mounting. Difficult as it was, she preferred to do it by herself so that no one would see her. First, she would have to lead the gentle horse up to a tree stump or a rock. Then she would step on it and position herself carefully so that she could reach the stirrup with her left foot. Finally, she would pull herself up, the right foot dragging behind her, and use her remaining strength to swing her right leg over the palfrey's croup without hitting the horse.

It was all so difficult and unsightly that, were it not for the joy of riding, she would not do it at all. But once she was mounted, she could move, almost as freely as others did. For that, she would bear the pain.

But for him to see her…

The horse, well trained, ambled over to the log on her signal. If she asked, politely, would Nicholas look away and spare her the embarrassment?

She took a breath to ask him, but before she could speak he lifted her up, close enough to the saddle that she could find her seat, then it was easy to pull her right leg into position and settle in the saddle.

All done so quickly that she had no time to worry about how she looked. And so smoothly that their bodies did not linger together long enough to allow temptation again.

'I thank you.' Words she hated to say, yet he deserved them.

A quick glance, as if he were as unaccustomed to receiving thanks as she was to giving them.

'You are kind to say so,' he said, solemn as if she had taken an oath.

'Usually, no one…' She let the words trail off. She had been helped by servants, pages, or even squires on occasion, but never by a gentleman.

He studied her with eyes that seemed to look deeper than she wanted.

'Let us go,' he said, finally, mounting his own horse. 'And hear the King's tales of how he killed the stag.'

No. She was not invisible to this man. And that made him even more dangerous.

Chapter Six

They returned to the lodge and Anne retreated to the chamber next to her lady's, glad of a chance to rest her leg until the hunting party returned and Lady Joan called for her.

Her lady had a maid, of course, to help her out of her garments, but to Anne fell the honour of combing her lady's hair.

Thus their days would end, with Anne allowed to sit behind her lady, a concession to Anne's condition. Then, as Anne combed the long, blonde locks, first with the thick side of the comb, Lady Joan would chatter of her day's delights. Once in a while, she would ask Anne what she had observed of this lady or that knight.

No, Anne could not run or walk, but she could watch and listen. And that, in and of itself, was a talent.

So Anne would talk and Joan would listen—one of the few times she *did* listen—and tuck each bit of information away, only to pull it out later, to use as one might offer a treat to a dog to lure him to her lap. Or, she might express a similar opinion, one she already knew the hearer held. At that, the man—and it was almost always a man—would be delighted and think her the most wonderful woman and one who understood him completely.

Lady Joan soon returned to the lodge, eyes bright and cheeks flushed from the hunt. She sat down in front of the mirror and Anne placed herself behind her, ready to start combing her mistress's hair.

'Did you enjoy the hunt, my lady?'

She lifted her shoulders. 'I do it because Edward likes it. He shot the stag so his father owes him for the wager they made. And so, a happy day.'

'A joyful day indeed, my lady.' Words by rote.

Joan glanced back over her shoulder, pulling her heavy hair out of Anne's hand. 'And your hunt? What more have you learned of Sir Nicholas?'

That was the reason, the only reason, that she had ridden beside Nicholas today. So she could answer that question.

'He has no lady, so he needs no gift for her.' And he was not likely to have one, if she judged him right. 'He holds a French hostage and he plans to return to fighting when he has discharged his duty to the Prince.'

And he kissed me.

But her lady must not know about the kiss.

Lady Joan nodded, absently, and turned forward. 'The King's messenger returned.'

Anne picked up the comb again and let loose a breath, slowly, so as not to betray her relief. Her lady was satisfied. There would be no more questions about Sir Nicholas tonight. 'So soon? I thought it would take near a fortnight to travel to Canterbury and back.'

'He did not go so far. He met some travellers who reported there is no pestilence between here and there.'

'So when will Sir Nicholas leave? Tomorrow?' She prayed it would be so. Every minute that she shared a roof with the man seemed a threat.

'I think so. Edward said he would go, too, but I don't want him to. No reason for him to risk the plague. Sir Nicholas steered the Pope to our side. He can certainly handle the Archbishop.' She looked back at Anne with an assessing eye and smiled. 'Come. Let me comb your hair.'

'It is my task to comb yours, my lady.' Uneasy, to be treated with such kindness from Lady Joan.

'Ah, but you are ever so patient with my little foibles. Come. Turn around.'

So Anne pulled a few blonde strands from the teeth on the side of the comb made for thick hair and discarded them, then handed the comb to Lady Joan. 'You'll need use only the thin side, my lady.'

An uneasy feeling at first, to have her lady at her back, where Anne could not read her every expression. Yet the gentle tug, the soft hands, the few moments of peace spun around her, as if Joan's calming presence itself touched her head and shoulders. As long as she stayed close, she was wrapped in Joan's world, where everything would be as it must.

'Your hair is lovely, Anne.'

It wasn't. It was thin and pale red, like a garment too often washed, but her lady was ever kind. 'Thank you, my lady.'

'Hold up the glass,' Lady Joan said. 'Take a look.'

As she did, Anne could see the two of them reflected there. Even though Lady Jane was eight years older, it was her face that held the eye.

She wondered what Nicholas thought of it.

Yet her lady was pointing to Anne's face next to hers in the glass.

'You are young still.'

Younger than Joan, though Anne did not remind her.

And Joan did not pause to note it. 'True, your hair is more red than fair, your mouth is too wide, your cheeks and hands have lost a maiden's purity.'

She glanced at her fingers, rubbing the callous earned by her stitches. If her hands were not as white and soft as Joan's, there was a reason for it.

'But your brow is broad and fair. If we plucked this stray hair here, touched your cheek with safflower powder to give a glow—'

Anne near dropped the mirror. 'Those things will not disguise my leg.'

'No, but you may yet catch a man's eye.'

She laughed then, that laugh she had perfected. Anne could delight the ear, if not the eye. 'Do you think to rid yourself of me, my lady?'

'Of course, not. I promised your mother…' She did not finish the sentence. There was no need. 'But I am so happy, with Edward. I want you to find a husband, too.'

Anne had seen all the scenes of love and lust and of marital contentment, knowing that none of it would be for her. A man might wed a plain woman for money or because she could help raise children and run the household. He might bed a beautiful one for love or lust.

But a lame one was of little use to anyone. Except, perhaps, to God.

But Anne had never wanted the cloistered life, shut away from the world's delights…

'Perhaps another pilgrimage,' Lady Joan began.

She shook her head. Her mother had petitioned God in the beginning. As soon as she had risen from the bed of childbirth, she had travelled to the shrine of the Blessed Larina, carrying her babe, hoping for a miracle. Larina did not grant it. Neither did St Winifred, St Werburgh, St Etheldreda, or the Virgin herself.

The miracle she was given was not a cure. It was the protection of Lady Joan.

One could not question God's wisdom.

'No, I am certain of it.' Lady Joan said as she rose, leaving half of Anne's hair uncombed, and paced the chamber. 'A pilgrimage to Canterbury. God will give you a miracle.'

Where had such a strange idea come from? Joan

had never spoken of curing her before. 'My lady, I don't think—'

'And you can go right away. Tomorrow! With Sir Nicholas Lovayne!'

She near laughed again, and not with mirth, trying to fight the desire that the thought raised. To stay beside Nicholas for a few more days, living in hope and fear that he might want to...

'Sir Nicholas does not need to be burdened with me when he must resolve the Pope's request about your wedding.'

Nicholas, he had made clear, did not want to be burdened with anyone. Even a wife.

Then Joan looked at her again, directly, smiling, the horn comb keeping a steady rhythm against her palm. 'You will be no burden to him. And you will be a great help to me.'

And then, she knew. She would not be travelling to Canterbury in hopes of a cure. She would be travelling as a spy for Lady Joan.

Nicholas was still thinking of Anne that evening as he prepared to leave, despite all efforts to put her out of his mind. He had done his duty. Been kind. He had no further obligation. The kiss? A mistake she had been gracious enough to ignore.

So would he.

Tomorrow he would ride to Canterbury, free, without needing to look back in fear she had fallen off the horse.

And when a page came to summon him to her

side, he told himself it was not so strange. She must only want to thank him again and bid him farewell.

But when he saw her, sitting on the garden bench in the fading light, squinting over her stitching, the set of her lips and her chin did not bode well.

'Are you recovered from the hunt?'

She nodded and lifted her head. Her fingers stilled. 'What time do you leave tomorrow?'

'At daybreak. The trip is long and the time short.'

'Send a page when you are ready. I shall be going with you.'

He could not have heard right. 'What?'

'I travel with you.'

'Why?' His words lacked grace, but his tongue had learned to be blunt in her presence.

She looked away, briefly. 'It is not...I do not expect...'

There. Both of them tongue-tied. The kiss, the fact of it lay between them.

She lifted her chin again, the weak moment gone. 'We will not be alone.'

Of course, there would be a retinue, small, but one that dignified the importance of the journey.

'No. We will not.' But temptation was not his only objection. He remembered her struggle to mount and dismount. He had no time for that now. 'I know you wanted to travel, but I must—'

'Move quickly. I know. We have already lost time waiting for the messenger.'

She was a sensible woman and she knew she would weigh him down. Then why? Suspicion stirred. Had the kiss misled her? A smile exchanged, some pleasant words, but surely she did not think it meant more than that.

Or did she?

Her loyalty was to her lady. That would be his appeal. 'I'm sure Lady Joan cannot spare you at this time with all the preparations to be made. For the wedding.' An argument certain to sway.

'It was her idea that I go. She thought, perhaps, a pilgrimage…' She would not meet his eyes.

A pilgrimage. Hope once more for a cure.

Guilt wrestled with duty. How could he refuse this woman, or anyone so afflicted, the hope of a visit to the shrine of a saint? Yet the journey to Canterbury would take at least seven days, though he had hoped to push the horses faster. That would be impossible if she rode with him.

He swallowed a sharp retort and searched for careful words. 'So you have not gone before? On pilgrimage?'

She shook her head. 'No. My mother did. More than once when I was small and then…' she shrugged. 'We did not go again.'

And still she limped. 'Why do you think this time will be different?'

She flinched, his blunt words a blow. 'I do not. But Lady Joan always believes that all will be…

'…as it must.' He spoke the words with her.

She smiled. He didn't.

'Yes, exactly.'

So now, Lady Joan, with a woman's disregard

for any needs but her own, had tossed the burden of Anne's hope to him, expecting him to catch and juggle it without dropping responsibility for her own happiness.

And if he did not walk away this minute, he would say something he'd regret. 'I must see to the horses and supplies.' He had no time to waste arguing. He would lay the matter before Edward, tell him it was impossible to take Anne, and let the man handle his own wife. 'And find the Prince.'

He turned on his heel without another word.

'I think,' she said, words floating over his shoulder, 'that the Prince may surprise you.'

He did not look back. It was Anne of Stamford who would be surprised.

Nicholas found the Prince at dice, collecting from a winning throw, in a better mood than he had feared.

The Prince and his lady were sleeping separately now, as the Pope had ordered, and Edward was counting the days until they could be wed again. He would brook no delay in getting official approval, even if Anne believed otherwise.

'My lord, we leave at dawn.'

Smiling, Edward clasped Nicholas on the shoulder. 'Godspeed, my friend. Safe and speedy travels.'

'But you are joining me.'

He shook his head. 'You need no help from me. Joan and I will look forward to seeing you back again soon.'

A trip well planned unravelling before it had begun. Was it faith in Nicholas or fear of the pestilence that held him back? No, the explanation was probably simpler. What had Anne called it? *Want*. The undoing of many men, including his father.

'My travels will not be as swift as I had planned. One of Lady Joan's ladies thinks to travel with me.'

He was gratified to see the Prince look surprised. 'Who? Why?'

'Anne.' He put an upward lilt at the end of her name, as if he were unsure of it. 'Hoping for a cure for her leg. She said Lady Joan suggested it.'

Edward met Nicholas's frown with a smile. 'How kind my wife is. Always thinking of others.'

This was not going as he had hoped. Did love make all men such fools? 'Do you want her to go to the shrine or do you want your answer quickly?'

Edward's frown was brief. 'If Joan wants her to go, then go she shall. I have every faith that you can handle one lame woman as well as the Archbishop. It can be no more difficult than the four hogsheads of Gascon wine you had to smuggle out of the priests' quarters in St Thierry.'

He wished, for a moment, that the Prince had less faith in him. Here was where Nicholas's pride had led. He made it look so easy, so Edward did not understand the difficulties.

Or did not admit that he did.

While he was still marshalling arguments for the Prince, he found himself, by force of habit, revising travel plans, recalculating the number of days on the road.

'I can take her there and bring her back,' he said, 'but whether she limps or runs afterwards is in God's hands, not mine.'

Edward shook his head. 'Poor maid. Joan took her on when others would not and keeps her ever close. What a treasure is my wife. How kind and gentle...'

Nicholas let the Prince ramble. Kind to this lame woman beyond what he would expect of any mortal. Well, everyone seemed to love the Lady Joan.

Joan took her on... And Anne had never answered when he asked how long she had been in her service. Would she know something of this marriage tangle he'd been given to unravel?

'How long?' he asked, cutting off the Prince in mid-sentence. 'How long have they been together?'

Edward shrugged. 'At least fifteen years. Her mother served Joan before her.'

'So when Joan was still married to Salisbury?'

That brought a frown. The Prince did not care to be reminded that he would be the third man to share his wife's marital bed. 'It is of no importance to your duty to take her there and back.'

No, he thought, but it was curious. It was a long, long time. 'And her father?'

'Died with honour in France. But why do you ask? These questions will not get you to Canterbury and back any faster.'

And that, of course, was all that concerned the Prince.

Nicholas bowed and left the room. If Anne had been with her lady so long, she had been there not only for their wedding, but also when Holland had appeared to reclaim his wife.

Strange, that Anne had never mentioned that.

Chapter Seven

Nicholas watched, wary, as Anne appeared promptly the next morning, garbed and prepared for travel. Did he see a sly glance? A wistful sigh? Any sign that she expected to return from this journey with a husband instead of a cure?

'You understand,' he began, in his sternest tone, 'that we do not have time for you to walk to Canterbury.'

Cruel words. Chosen to keep her safely distant.

That hard edge in her eyes again. 'I am lame. I am not an idiot.'

Hardly words to entice a man's sensual imaginings.

He gritted his teeth. She had that habit. Each time a wave of guilt seemed about to crash over him, she would say something pointed and sharp enough to prick him with anger instead of pity.

For that, he was thankful. It kept him from thinking of her in other ways.

'Nor,' he continued, 'have we time for you to make your will, or give away your worldly goods, or be blessed at mass, or any of the rest of it.'

A proper pilgrimage was near as ritualised as the mass or the stag hunt. There was a long list of things God demanded before he would bestow his mercy.

'If you are warning me not to blame you if the saint does not cure me, do not worry. My prayers, and my mother's, have been ignored up to this time. I don't think one more blessing will make a difference to St Thomas one way or another.'

'Then why go at all?'

She made no quick retort this time and, in the silence, his suspicions resurfaced. Was there something more to this journey than she had said?

Finally, she blinked, as if waking from a distant vision. 'I have not been away from Lady Joan in more than fifteen years.'

A startling thought. The royal household was constantly on the move. By the time he was ready to return from Canterbury, the King would have moved on to Clarendon or Brockenhurst or Carisbrooke. Individual members of the household might stay behind or go before. For Anne to have never been separated from her lady in so long was more than unusual.

He could not imagine that kind of constancy. But her affliction, of course, made any travel monumental, best undertaken with a cart to move her. Travelling with Lady Joan, they could ride together in safety and comfort.

For her to come on this journey, on horseback,

accompanied by only a few knights and squires and a maid, must take more courage than he had appreciated. 'Will you miss her?'

She smiled. 'I'll have time to discover that, won't I?'

And he saw no fear in her eyes. Only a yearning that rekindled the twinge of weakness he had felt in his chest more than once when he looked at her.

He struggled to reclaim his stern face, searched for curt words.

Oh, a quick kiss with a smiling maiden was a harmless diversion when he was stuck in the New Forest for three days. They had shared some barbed words and some laughter, but he had always known he would move on.

Yet now, when he was ready to leave, here she was. And here she would be, day after day, on the road beside him.

And what was worse, was that he was not certain he minded.

Anne had journeyed on horseback before, but never for so long a ride, day after day. Roads were rutted, carts slow and uncomfortable, and sometimes, she and her lady had been carried in the comfort of a litter, cushioned with pillows and shielded from wind and sun.

There would be no such respite now.

Simply to stay on the horse took all her strength. Her right foot could not rest in the stirrup, so she clenched her thighs, as tightly as she could, hoping with every mile that she would not slide off and be trampled. The horse, sensing her tension, seemed to fight her, making every step a struggle.

By afternoon, her muscles shook with pain.

Yet she felt happy enough to sing.

Though she had imagined, in the moments before sleep, journeying to the far corners of the world, seeing sights too strange to be imagined, she knew it to be a dream. Only in the circle of her lady's protection could she live safely. In lucid, waking moments, she could not conceive of leaving Lady Joan's side.

Yet here she was, on a lovely summer day, so far away she could not hear or see or even be summoned by the Countess. And instead of fear, exhilaration pulsed through her. She took in the wonderful scent of flowers, first those of bright yellow, then some of vivid blue, and the rise and fall of the grasslands at the edge of the forest. Perhaps they would ride near enough to the water that she would get a glimpse.

Happiness—all the result of a freedom she had never known. Because now, today, she could pretend she was the person she wanted to be, one who could travel unencumbered. That was the reason. Not Sir Nicholas Lovayne.

His horse inched ahead of her time after time and he kept looking over his shoulder as if to make sure she still kept her seat.

Abruptly, he rode closer, as if he had recognised her thought. They had not spoken since she had mounted, a process made easy with his help. He had a way of lifting her so gracefully that it was no longer a struggle to get on the horse.

'Is it comfortable for you?' he said. 'To ride? Should we stop to rest?'

Kind of him to ask. He had not seemed so generous this morning. And even if she had to tie herself to the horse, she would not succumb. 'You said it yourself. We have no time. Besides, isn't a pilgrim supposed to suffer?' She smiled, as if to assure him she did not.

She hoped he did not see her grit her teeth.

'Come. Let us rest and eat.'

He gave quick orders to those with them and his squire Eustace scurried to set up a blanket while Agatha, the serving girl Lady Joan had lent her, unpacked a cold meal by the stream. They travelled lightly, escorted by only two knights and their squires.

But Nicholas arranged everything, a task much simpler, she was certain, than managing food and drink for hundreds of men, as he had in France. Still, with him, she was not a lady-in-waiting with an obligation to fetch or carry.

He came to the near side of her horse, ready to lift her down and she braced herself against desire.

His arms were strong and tight. Then her body pressed to his, close, close as lovers might be. But there was nothing beyond duty in his care of her. She knew that. He was the Prince's man, she attached to Lady Joan. But somehow, away from the court, no longer surrounded, she felt as if they had escaped for a tryst.

Her feet touched the uneven ground and she stumbled, leaning into him so she would not fall.

'I have you.' His voice was a rumble in his chest. 'Don't worry.'

She closed her eyes, only to see a fantasy she had long forbidden herself.

The picture of herself as an ordinary woman. One who might have a husband, even a lover. If she were that woman, would she choose this man? Surely she was attracted only because he was the one man who had come near enough to touch her.

She raised her eyes, murmuring thanks, and was struck by him all over again.

Tall and straight, yes. That she had known from the first. He was of a similar height to the King or the Prince. Unusual. Few men could look either Edward in the eye. Nicholas stood on equal ground.

With her hands on his arms she could feel the strength that could swing a sword, yet his muscles, like so much about him, seemed hidden, used as a last resort instead of a first. Finely carved lips were a sharp contrast to a nose that looked as if it had lived through more than one battle. Taken together, he was an uneasy mix of diplomat and warrior.

She raised her eyes to meet his, so deep set it was hard to see their colour or read his expression. Too late, she realised he was gazing back at her.

'What are you looking at?' he said.

'Your eyes.' Too late to lie.

He leaned back, near dropping her, but he did not look away. 'And your conclusion?'

Heat bloomed on her cheek and crept lower. Could he see her thoughts?

No. Certainly not. And if he were strong enough to hold her gaze, she would not look away. 'I thought your eyes were brown, but I was wrong. They are…'

She narrowed her gaze. She had never been able to name the colour of his eyes. Green or brown in this light, then grey and gold when she looked again. Certainty elusive as a feather, lifted by the wind just out of reach, as hard to describe as the man himself.

'Anne? What?'

How long had she gazed into his eyes, as if she were attempting a seduction? 'I do not know. Just when I am ready to say green or blue, I look again and all has changed.'

Now, a smile in truth. 'That has been helpful to me when I must bargain.'

Ah, yes. Eyes that seemed to show a glimpse of his soul, but instead, only hid it. 'What colour do you call them?' A light and careless question. One that might be asked by a woman who could dance.

He blinked, as if her question surprised him. 'I cannot see my own eyes. Nor do I gaze at myself in a glass. Why do you want to know?'

Because I want to know everything about you.

For her lady's sake alone, of course. But she could not say so. Better he think that she played at seduction, lightly, no more serious than the games ladies played with men after dinner in the Hall. Nothing that suggested there was any connection between this and his kiss…

'Your mother, then. What colour did she call them?'

Pain. Anger. Something more. And then, his gaze took hers again. 'What colour would you call yours?'

'Mine?' She glanced at the looking glass as often as most, she supposed, but never deeply. 'I don't study my own eyes.'

'Well, neither do I.' The set of his lips told her he would say no more.

She reached for her stick, an excuse to look away. To think. The others had already gathered on the blanket to share bread and cheese, but suddenly, the yards between here and there seemed impossibly long.

She took two steps, three. Then her legs, shaking from a morning's tight grip on the horse, refused to carry her further and she sank onto the remains of a broken stone wall.

'Stay,' he said. 'I'll bring something to you.'

Relieved, she allowed him to fetch and carry for her. He returned with bread, cheese and ale. To Anne's surprise, he sat beside her as she ate.

'So you've been with Lady Joan fifteen years,' he began.

'How did you know that?'

He raised an eyebrow. 'Because this morning, you said you had not been away from her in so long.'

How could she have been so foolish? She munched on her bite of bread longer than necessary, wondering how to turn the question away. On the blanket, Eustace and Agatha sat side by side, heads close together.

'So,' she said, briskly, brushing the crumbs off her fingers, 'since neither of us can name the colour of our own eyes, you will tell me what colour mine are and I'll tell you what colour yours are.'

A diversion to keep him from asking questions about the past. She leaned toward him and stared into his eyes, opening hers wide, as if to give him a good look, then made her lashes flutter like bird's wings.

He tried to look stern, but chuckled instead. 'I am surprised to hear you sound so light-hearted.'

She had his attention. Now, she must keep it. 'Oh, come now, Sir Knight. Have you never gazed deeply into a woman's eyes?' A question only meant to distract him. Not asked because she cared to know.

He tamed the smile and gazed into her eyes, but with a serious, thoughtful expression that threatened no repeat of kisses. 'Your eyes are grey. And…green, too.'

Grey. Green. No poesy there.

'And yours, now. Let me see.' His eyes were hidden, somehow. Shadowed by a brow and eyelids that looked as if he were perpetually assessing you, so that you could not see him. 'Yours are the blue-grey of a cloud, hiding the light of the moon.'

He shook his head. 'I have not seen you so… *volage* before.'

She felt *volage*. As light and giddy as Agatha's laughter, floating on the summer breeze, and she wasn't sure whether she was acting so because she was away from the life she knew or because she was trying to distract him or because with him she felt…

different. 'Too much fresh air, perhaps. Or perhaps it is…'

You.

She bit her lip against the word.

Meanwhile, there he was. Assessing her with a tilted head, a slight furrow between the strong, straight brows and pursed lips.

She looked away. She lacked any skill with men. She should not have tried to be what she was not. 'You look as if you are assessing a horse to see if it is worthy of being ridden by a King's man.' And then she felt her cheeks heat. Ridden. As a man might ride a maid… 'I did not mean—'

Worse, now. Suddenly, the cloud over his eyes shifted, as if the moon had been revealed, and she seemed to see clearly what he saw. Him. Her. Together. Looking at her the way she had seen men looking at women they desired. Men had not gazed at her that way.

They had not gazed at her at all.

And though she should not have, she turned back to meet his eyes again, hungry to glimpse that desire, if only for a moment. No, she would not have the bliss of the Prince and her lady, but just this taste…

The clouds returned. 'Neither did I.' Cutting off the thought as thoroughly as she had tried to do.

There was something behind the clouds, though. Something sharp and bright and clear that spoke of the distant lands he had travelled. Of sights, sounds, and scents she could not begin to understand.

And would never see.

He rose and held out a hand. 'Come. We must ride again. I will arrange a harness to hold you, so you can ride more easily.'

After that, Nicholas kept his distance. He devised a belt and strap of rope and leather to keep her more secure. With that, she and the horse seemed to settle and he no longer had to look over his shoulder every moment in fear she had fallen to the road. He showed the other knights, even the squires, how to help her on and off the horse, but by the next day, he could no longer bear to watch their inept attempts. The men were clumsy with the fastenings as well as with her. If he did not step in, they would injure themselves and the horse as well as Anne.

So he took responsibility again, although it put him close to her near a dozen times a day. The gestures had become easy for him, but he performed them with stiff arms, trying to keep her body away from his.

And still he caught the scent of her hair, like some spicy forbidden fruit, hidden within a deep forest.

When that happened, he would tense his arms and she would stiffen her spine and although they touched, it was as if a wall of pavise shields stood between them, strong enough to ward off a shower of enemy arrows.

He told himself she was nothing more than an obstacle in his path, like a river in flood or a muddy road that must be traversed in order to keep moving, then left behind. Dealing with her physical limitations on the journey was no more difficult than persuading a

French baker to sell bread to the English enemy or finding a port near the fighting for the supply ships to dock. He had solved many more difficult challenges.

But those problems had come and gone and troubled him no more while thoughts of Anne never fully left him. Beyond the fact that he must answer for her safety and comfort, some mixture of resentment and concern, edged with unwelcome desire, hovered, always close.

Then, he would look at her and see her smile and that would make him happy, thinking he had somehow been responsible for it.

It would take near ten days to reach Canterbury, longer than if all the riders were able bodied. Nicholas pushed to keep the pace, all the while watching Anne when she was not looking at him.

Was she in pain? If so, she hid it well. Proud and stubborn. Determined not to slow them down.

They reached Winchester by the end of the second day. He sent his squire and the others to arrange rooms in the tavern while he took Anne to the Pilgrim's Hall, in the shadow of the Cathedral.

She would have little rest here, he thought, as she settled in, but at least she would be beneath a roof. Heavy wooden beams soared to an arched ceiling that seemed to imitate a cathedral. Yet there was none of the sanctuary's peace or quiet. The open room was crowded with pilgrims and travellers scattered across the floor, each seeking the illusion of separate space.

She would be safe here and he would be glad to

leave her for the night. If she were beyond his sight, he would certainly be able to sleep with untroubled dreams.

'You will be comfortable here,' he said, already thinking of what he would do if she said no.

'The court travels regularly,' she said, her self-sufficiency as strong as a suit of armour, though weariness shadowed her eyes and weighed on her shoulders. 'My serving girl is here. She can accompany me.'

'Accompany you?' Worry sharpened the words until they sounded like anger. 'Where?'

'I am going to Greyfriars Church.'

'Why?' He was tired. She must be exhausted. 'You agreed to forgo pilgrim duties.'

Her eyes met his. 'It is not part of my pilgrimage. The Earl of Kent is buried there. My lady asked that I visit his burial place.'

'Lady Joan's former husband? Was he not buried in France?'

'Not he. Her brother.'

'Brother?' If she insisted, he could not let her walk the streets with only a maid for company. A new, difficult path stretched between here and his pint of ale. 'Was he taken by the pestilence?' No one had mentioned the death of a brother.

She shook her head. 'He died nine years ago. At twenty-two.'

Twenty-two. Were the man still alive, he would be Nicholas's age. 'In war?' Had he known the Earl? Marched or fought beside him? He tried to remember.

That year had been a blur of truce and battle, back and forth between the Scots and the French. There had been so many marches, so many battles.

'No. He just…died. Who knows how death takes some men?'

He looked back at her, sharply. Was there more than loyalty in her devotion? 'Were you…fond on him?'

Wide eyes of shock. 'He was married.'

He did not bother to say how little that could mean. 'But you knew him?'

'Of course. He was Joan's last living brother. When he died, the land and the title became hers.'

That would not explain her loyalty. In his experience, women were not so selflessly devoted to others. Only to themselves. Still, if she'd had a fondness for a man once, it was her own secret and no concern of his. He had become fanciful. Her reasons mattered not. He only had to deal with the consequences.

'Your devotion to your lady is admirable.' His jealous response to a dead man was not.

She grimaced, proof he had not fooled her. 'Have you never been loyal to someone?'

'To Edward and the King, of course.' Yet his loyalty to the Prince and his father joined with duty, obligation and survival. It was not this emotional bond she seemed to have. It was beyond gratitude.

'To no one else? Your family?'

'My family was not worth such devotion.' She had lived near all her life with her lady. He had left his own family behind years ago.

Dismay softened her face. 'I am sorry for that.'

'I'm ready.' The serving girl's voice surprised him. 'Eustace has said he will come with us.'

'No, he won't.' Eustace, he was certain, was only going to be with Agatha. The young idiot would be playing the man for her instead of caring for Anne. 'If you wish to visit the church, I will take you.'

'But I—'

'If any harm came to you, Lady Joan would have me drawn and quartered.' And so would the Prince, too, if his lady asked. He waved off the maid and the squire, who looked happy to be left to entertain each other, and handed Anne her staff. 'Here.'

As tired as they both were, Nicholas commandeered a cart so Anne would not have to walk or ride, pushed her through the streets to the church, helped her rouse one of the brothers to receive a new memorial gift from Lady Joan and watched as Anne prayed before the small memorial.

A full-size sculpture lay atop the coffin, as if the man had turned to stone on his deathbed.

A young, titled man, with lands. Gone.

Born the same year that Nicholas was, now he moved no more.

A chill from the stone floor crept into his feet and rose up his calves.

Death came when it would. Nicholas knew that as well as any man. Quickly or slowly, foreseen or unexpected, he was ready for it.

At least, that was what he had told himself.

Now, he wondered. When he died, there would be

nothing left. That was the life he had chosen. One with nothing that would weigh him down. No title or lands. No wife. No child. No one to mourn him.

Not even a member of the household, like loyal Anne of Stamford, to pause before the tomb to say a prayer for his soul.

Anne pushed herself to her knees and he gave her a hand to help her rise. And when she stood, still leaning on him, he saw that she wept.

Tears. From a woman who never yielded. Was she more closely related to the family than he knew? A bastard daughter and half-sister, perhaps? Did she weep for a brother, for some lost, hopeless love, or simply at the sadness of death? It made no difference to him now. He could not bear to see her cry.

Without thinking, he pulled her close, tucking her head against his shoulder, stroking her hair. She fitted against him, shoulder to toe, as if made to do so. He tightened his arms, feeling her breathing press against him, her tears, damp on his shoulder. How did a man comfort a woman?

He had never thought to ask.

Finally, she lifted her head, her huge eyes, fringed by those light red lashes, tangled in tears. His breath matched hers, still uneven, and if he just bent his head, touched his lips to her…

Instead, she was the one who reached up, put her arm around his neck and kissed him.

A kiss quick and as unexpected as an arrow from a hidden enemy. And near as deadly.

Unlike an arrow though, it did not stop him from

moving, but drove him closer, gripped by the urge to protect, share, join, fall into her, give her his strength and lean on hers.

Then, as suddenly as they had come, her lips were gone.

Wide-eyed, she met his gaze. The grey-green eyes that had seemed dreamy only a moment ago had come to. Still as frank and assessing as when he had first seen them, but with a new caution, a shame he had never thought to see.

This was not what he had expected from a woman in tears before a dead man's grave and not what he had expected of himself.

Now, he was the one unsteady on his feet, robbed of words. For a second, he'd felt something that was more than physical. Something that had touched the Nicholas inside, behind the face the world saw.

But he did not let her go.

Chapter Eight

Anne broke from his arms and sank to the floor, turning away from his eyes. 'Forgive me.' Her lips still burned, though she refrained from touching them. I...' She cleared her throat. 'I have not... It is... I'm not sure...'

She was tripping over the words just as she tripped over her feet. What had she done? What madness had seized her?

Seized both of them. For he did not rebuff her, not even as he let her go. No, she felt, for that moment, as a normal woman might, able to touch and kiss and love without facing revulsion. The closeness, mile after mile, was making her long for things she could not have.

Even her father had refused her his lap on the rare occasions he was home.

She rubbed the tears from her cheeks, then searched for her stick, feeling blind as well as lame, but it was Nicholas who found it and handed it to her.

He cleared his throat, keeping at arm's length from her, letting her find her balance again. 'Are you all right?'

She nodded. Yet that was only partly true, for she knew that both of them were now off balance, unsteady in whatever new ground they had just walked onto.

She would be better only when she could neither see nor hear him, nor catch his scent if he came too close. For now, the floor was a haven and she did not try to rise.

Words. She must find words to reassure him. 'I did not… I should not… I did not mean…'

'I did not understand how deeply you mourned for him.'

She released a breath, thankful that he assumed she wept for a dead man. She did not. Joan's brother had been gone near ten years. She had come because her lady asked it.

No, her tears were for her own weakness. She wept because she wanted, against all reason, a life that was impossible. And then, he took her into his arms and she wanted, oh, how she wanted…

And then, she took it. Another kiss. Just one more time. And she could pretend…

She must look at him. She must pretend, again, that there had been no kiss, no hope, no desire.

'You are kind,' she began, blinking against the unwelcome sting of tears. Kind in a way she did not want. She allowed such care from no one, for it only affirmed her limitations. Reminded her too often of what she could not do.

No, no, Anne. You can't, said her mother. *Not by yourself.*

Yet when someone helped, she must be grateful. Oh, so grateful.

'Thank you,' she said, at last, near choking on the words.

He did not answer.

And when she braved his eyes again, she was trapped by a long, deep gaze. One that seemed to see what she did not show, hear what she did not say.

'I do not need thanks.' How long had they looked at each other in silence between her words and his? 'Do you ever have a moment's thought for yourself?'

Angry words. As if she should.

How could she tell him that she was thinking of little but herself. Of how she craved his company like a flower craved the rain.

'In caring for my lady, I do care for myself.'

He shook his head. 'You are too loyal.'

He must not know how loyal. 'Yet you serve the Prince.'

'I do what I must.' There was a curiosity in his gaze. 'But you…'

Distract him. Her lady's voice, as clear as if she were in the room.

She leaned on her stick, refusing his hand, and struggled to her feet. 'What you must? Hold crying women?' Was her smile too brittle? She hoped he would not notice.

'No.' Again, he cleared his throat, as if he might find his voice hidden there. 'At least, not until now.'

Nor had he wanted to, she would wager.

She took a step and slipped. Once again, he caught her. But this time there was nothing but her frailty between them and she was Anne again.

The slick stone floor and steps of the church required her full attention until they emerged into the street, now bathed in twilight.

He lifted her into the cart, as effortlessly as he plucked her on and off the horse, and picked up the handles to push her through the streets.

'So what do you do, Sir Nicholas?' There must be no more tears or telling silence. 'When you are not helping a *demoiselle en détresse?*'

'I make problems go away,' he said, with a sigh she recognised all too well.

'Ah, I have done the same.'

'You?'

'Indeed. You supply armies. I must oversee this year's Yuletide livery.'

'Is that so difficult?'

It was clear from his tone that the man had no understanding as to the complexities. 'This year? Yes. What colour shall we choose? Princess Isabella's garb must normally be bettered only by her mother the Queen, but this year, Lady Joan will be Princess of Wales and rank above Isabella! Both must be pleased and neither offended.'

'How can new clothes offend?'

'The entire family must wear the same colour so

they look perfect standing together. Even the servants' livery must match. Yet blue flatters Joan and Isabella likes it not. Isabella wants yellow and Joan refuses. The Queen, hoping for peace, floats above, leaving Isabella's lady, Cecily, and I to go between them searching for a solution.'

Then, he laughed. A sound, she wagered, that was as unfamiliar to him as it was to her. 'Women! Thinking only of themselves. And I thought finding food and water for ten thousand men and thirty thousand horses was hard!'

She gritted her teeth against a tart response. At least she had found a topic to distract him. 'Provisioning knights and archers cannot be compared to satisfying two princesses. I am grateful that Lady Cecily and I can laugh together.'

And so she entertained him with stories of counting ells and ermine skins and made him laugh again. Their companionship returned to its rightful place and the comfortable distance was restored.

She must not let it slip again.

In the days between Winchester and Canterbury, Nicholas rode more slowly. Edward and Joan could wait another day to wed. He would not harm Anne to pay for their folly. Yet the journey was still hard and there was little time, or breath, to tarry and talk.

Nicholas, convinced that Anne could keep up, or that she wished to pretend she could, kept his distance. And if she was silent because she was battling pain, he pretended not to notice.

Safer for them both that way.

So, once again, he let Eustace or one of the others help her on and off the horse, even though the idiots treated her as if she were a sack of grain, instead of a woman, because he could not risk getting close to her again.

One moment crying for a dead man. The next, kissing one very much alive. Why?

But who knew why women did anything except for their own gain. In his experience, women's interest in him had been directly proportional to what he could offer them. The camp followers wanted a tent and extra food, so he had been the centre of flattery and offers he chose, usually, to refuse. Women who wanted a husband would parade before him, hoping to tempt his eye, until they discovered he could not provide the wanted wealth that would make a marriage worthwhile.

The truth was that while Anne's actions were a puzzle, Nicholas was more worried about his own. He had come so close to not letting her go at all. Every time he got close, something urged him to go deeper, to *know,* to *understand* this woman whose eyes had trapped him from the first moment.

Why did he find her so alluring? He couldn't even tell what colour her eyes were. He had decided they were grey, then she would turn and he would call them blue-green. Yet in another light….

And as he was studying her eyes, the drift of her eyebrow would lead him to the place where her hair grew, hiding her ear in a tantalising way…

And then he sighed, disgusted to find the miles had rolled by while he puzzled over something that mattered not at all, as if he actually cared about this woman.

He had owned little in life and wanted less. Horse, armour, work. Food and drink. Enough to keep body and soul bound to each other, but not enough to hold him down. Never anything that would keep him from moving along.

But none of these things were things he desired, craved, or longed for. He saw them with the same cool necessity that had made him effective at moving food and weapons. Make a plan. Expect obstacles. Assess and solve each one without letting emotion substitute for judgement.

At first, he had barely understood or recognised that he was feeling something for her. Certainly there was no reason for it. She was a woman beyond the blush of maidenhood. And he had slipped over thirty without noticing. As a companion of the Prince, it was easy *not* to notice. The Prince did not marry and so neither one of them had crossed the line that somehow changed one's life, even if a man thought it would not.

And how did he come to think of marriage when he was thinking of Anne?

Yet he had thought of nothing but marriage, clandestine or real, for the last four months. At the end of all this, there would be a wedding, a ceremony, a celebration. That must be the reason his thoughts had turned to her, for his attraction to this woman was ridiculous and inexplicable.

And impossible to ignore.

All the better that his time with her would be brief.

In his head, Nicholas knew the reasons Anne wanted to make a pilgrimage, but only as they approached the West Gate of Canterbury did he realise, in his heart, why she was there.

Oh, he had seen pilgrims before now. Beggars. The blind, the dumb, the lame. Those without the ability that he had to move through the world. But not until today, not until he saw them littering the roadside like so many dead leaves, did he fully understand.

She could have been one of them.

Shocking as that thought was, the next one surprised him even more.

He had never really seen her that way. Not even from the first.

He stole a look at her, on the horse beside him. She kept her chin up and her eyes straight ahead, refusing to look down at the unfortunate souls. First, he wondered at her insensitivity. Then, he recognised something else. Day after day, she stayed atop the horse by pure force of will. Even with the harness, her legs were shaking with the pain of holding herself upright, all so she would not be left in the dirt like these people.

No, she did not see herself that way either.

Such courage dwarfed anything he had seen on the battlefield. It humbled him. Once, he had been ready to discard her as a burden. Instead, his doubts had been the burden. She would not suffer pity for herself, nor spare it for others. She certainly did not want it from him. She wanted nothing from him at all.

Except a kiss…

Their arrival at the inn was a welcome interruption to that thought. Now he must settle seven travellers and their horses, send word to the Archbishop of his arrival and attend to the multitude of other details that filled his days.

He made certain she was comfortable in the public room and it was an hour or more before he returned to see her still sitting there, in the corner where he had left her, looking out on to the street filled with the blind, the lame and the sick.

Crying.

Tears again, welling up in her eyes, overflowing, dripping down her cheeks and then splattering onto the wool dress, as steady as spring rain.

He stepped between her and the rest of the room, shielding her from prying eyes, and rested a hand on her shoulder.

'Are you…well?' Gruff words. Tripping over something lodged in his throat.

Anne turned sharply, as if he had attacked. 'Well? Am I well?' He heard the pain rip through her words. Pain she'd always hidden before.

But now that it had escaped, her words ran too quickly to be stopped. 'I am warm and dry and fed and cared for, unlike these poor creatures. And through no good of my own but only that of my lady.'

My lady. Of course. The reason for the depth of her

devotion was so clear, so obvious, that he had missed it. She owed her life to Lady Joan.

Have you never been loyal to anyone?

No. Not in that way. For him, loyalty was a manageable exchange. His arm, his sword, his skills, in exchange for money. Oh, it used to be that men pledged their lives and received protection in return, but now war had grown too large. Too many men had to take the field for too long. Only coins could keep the army in motion. Coins for the men and coins for the horses, arms and food to keep the men fighting.

'But you serve her well,' he began. Surely there must be a similar trade in her relationship with Lady Joan, not merely charity. 'It is not as if she gives you alms.' How demeaning that would be for a woman as proud as Anne.

She flinched, as if his words had been cruel.

Not his intent, but perhaps they were. After all, what could Anne offer Lady Joan in return for her protection? Beautifully stitched purses? Mediation on the colour of the Yuletide livery? Care of the children in off hours? Nothing that would ever equal what Lady Joan had given her. Her life.

Her tears had stopped and she shook her head. 'No, it is worse than that. I—'

The words stopped and her expression changed, as completely as if a veil had covered her face. And once more, she was the Anne he knew, a woman proud, stubborn and strong.

Everything else was hidden.

* * *

Beneath the table, Anne wove her fingers tightly together and closed her eyes, giving prayerful thanks to God that she had stopped herself before she told this man everything he must not know.

What a weak, spineless woman she had become. Just a few days of being close enough to touch a man, close enough to dream, and she had forgotten who she really was.

'Anne?'

Now. I must look at him as I always do. I must give him no reason to question.

She opened her eyes, only to see Canterbury's crowded streets again, full of pilgrims with wounds visible and invisible. Turning her back, she faced Nicholas. 'Forgive me. Being here, surrounded like this, I was…overcome.'

Her lady and her mother and the secret. That was all that stood between her and those wretched creatures.

His hand, she realised, still cradled her shoulder and he squeezed it, a gesture that seemed more intimate than any kiss they had shared. 'I am sorry. This, I cannot make right.'

Simple words that nearly undid her. When had anyone ever told her such a thing?

Her fingers met his. 'You are a kinder man than you think, Sir Nicholas Lovayne.'

To her relief, he straightened, breaking the intimacy. 'And you are a gentler woman than you show, Anne of Stamford.'

No, she was not. She was a woman who knew something that must be kept from Sir Nicholas Lovayne at any cost.

A smile now. 'All will be as it must.' She waved him away. 'Go. You must not worry.'

You must not become curious or suspicious or ask more questions.

For keeping that secret had been, simply, the reason for her life. Now, she would keep it for another reason.

She would keep it so that the caring she had seen in his grey-blue eyes, caring she had never seen from another person, would not turn to abomination.

And as he left to make arrangements for the beds and the horses, she gazed after him, choking on truths she dare not speak.

I am not the woman you think I am. I am a woman whose life is based on a lie and I hope you never discover the truth about me.

Nicholas forced himself to leave Anne and plunge into the distraction of the mundane. Let the serving girl attend her. He needed distance, needed to rend that invisible tie that kept pulling him to her.

Exactly the sort of tie he never wanted.

That was what had trapped his father into marriage with a second wife. There had been no logic, no reason to the choice. And later, all of them had regretted it, even the woman who had blinded his father to the truth.

But at the time, his father, full of love—longing—could think of nothing but this woman.

Nicholas would never make that mistake. Not with anyone. Certainly not with Anne of Stamford.

Kind, she called him. No, he was not kind. He was not given to passions of any sort.

Many were. Men like the Prince and his father roared with laughter or anger, loved who or what they would. They let their swords escape their brains and rode into battle blinded with blood lust instead of the sharp, clear-eyed calm needed in order to stay alive. They killed or maimed or, conversely, gifted friends with presents worth a ransom, acting as an animal might, with no more control than a squalling babe. He had never been a man like that. His father's life had taught him well.

Instead, he watched. He assessed. He investigated. He planned. Only then did he act. And when something went wrong, and something always went wrong, he reassessed and adjusted.

There was always another way, a different choice, if you took the time to think instead of letting fear or desire overcome judgement.

And if frustration or anger sometimes choked him, he swallowed it and moved on. It was his strength, this control. It had kept him far away from the dangers of too much anger.

Or too much love.

The spectre of the dead man in Winchester rose to haunt him again. Dead. Gone. With nothing to show he had lived on this earth.

Yet that was what Nicholas had chosen. A life with nothing to weigh him down or hold him back. And when it was over, he would leave nothing behind.

That was the way he had always wanted it.

And still did.

Chapter Nine

The next morning after prayers, Nicholas was ushered into the Cathedral Priory and admitted to the office of Simon Islip, the Archbishop of Canterbury.

As he dropped to his left knee and kissed the offered ring, Nicholas turned an assessing eye on the Archbishop. He was, as the Prince had said, in his seventh decade, and as stern and prickly a character as one would expect the highest church official in the realm to be.

Nicholas rose.

They eyed each other warily.

Nicholas had youth on him. That was a comfort. He only hoped the stubborn old man's mind could summon up the memories he needed.

In well-rehearsed words, Nicholas conveyed the King's respects and the Pope's request, careful to keep the impatience from his voice. The journey itself was no doubt the most difficult part of this assignment and that was half-done. All he needed now was for the Archbishop's clerk to find the document so that the man could mutter his blessing over it. Then, the only thing standing between Nicholas and France would be the English Channel.

He finished speaking and waited. The Archbishop's face did not waver. Nor did he speak.

'We do this at the request of His Holiness,' Nicholas said, finally, wondering whether the man had heard him at all.

Now, the lips twisted a bit. 'The French Pope?'

He blinked, somewhat surprised. Typically, such words were not said aloud. 'And the request of His Grace the King.'

Islip had not always bowed to the royal will. Despite that, or maybe because of it, the King respected him.

The Archbishop waved a hand. 'A man grows old. His tongue grows loose.' Beneath greying brows, his blue eyes took on a distant look. 'God has taken the bishops of Worcester, London and Ely with the pestilence. How am I to replace such men?'

The Archbishop had his own concerns, as all men did. It was Nicholas's task to overcome them. 'The Prince asked that I help you in any way I can. As you can understand, he wants all to be in order when the official dispensation arrives for he is eager to be wed.'

'A little too eager,' Islip snapped. 'Now he expects us to be just as eager.'

Nicholas had the uneasy feeling that the man would have said the same if he had spoken to Prince Edward himself. 'I believe,' Nicholas said in as calm a tone as he could muster, 'that all that must be done is to locate the document, review it and issue a statement. I am sure that is what His Holiness expects.' His Holiness had barely allowed enough time for them to complete even that simple task.

'*All* that he expects? To locate and examine a document from when?'

'Fourteen years ago.' That was when the appeal for the dissolution of Joan's marriage to Salisbury had gone to the Pope and the legitimacy of her clandestine marriage to Holland had been upheld.

Fourteen years. Before the Death. Before this man was Archbishop. Before Nicholas had been knighted. He tried to remember himself then, at seventeen. Attached to the Prince's household, yes, but more interested in the newly founded Order of the Garter and more fearful of the impending plague than interested in the marriage, or lack thereof, of the King's cousin.

The Archbishop dropped his forehead into his hands and rubbed his eyes, as if the years he battled against had suddenly settled upon him. 'Explain it to me again,' he said, with a sigh. 'About the marriage.'

Nicholas could understand the man's confusion. It had taken several tellings before even he had grasped the complexities.

'As I understand it,' he began, 'the Lady Joan and Thomas Holland conducted a clandestine marriage between them when she was twelve. After that, he went off to war. A few months later, her mother forced her to marry the Earl of Salisbury.'

'When she was already married?'

'Exactly.' It sounded impossible, stated so simply.

'How could she consent to such a thing? Did she not tell them she was wed in the eyes of God?'

The same questions had nipped at Nicholas, but he had stifled them. 'I cannot say what the Lady Joan might have said to her mother or to Salisbury.' Or to the King and Queen, who had taken responsibility for their distant cousin when her father died.

Islip sighed. 'So this lady, married already, married another man with her family's permission. What happened then?'

'When Holland returned to England, he asserted his claim of a prior marriage and took it to the Pope, who agreed.'

'Which Pope?'

How was he to know? And what difference did it make? Nicholas was beginning to wonder whether the situation was too complex for a man of Islip's age to understand. 'It took two years for the petition to be granted, so twelve years ago.'

'Pope Clement.'

Well, that part of the man's memory worked well enough. 'Pope Clement. So now, Pope Innocent wants verification that all was in order with the dissolution of the marriage to Salisbury before Lady Joan and the Prince wed.'

The Archbishop leaned back in his high-backed chair and crossed his arms. 'Let me see if I understand this. Lady Joan had a clandestine marriage to one man, then a legitimate marriage to a different man. So she was, at one time, married to two different men.'

The baldest way to look at it. No surprise that the

Prince's desire to make the woman his wife had led to whispers across the kingdom. 'You could say so.'

'Was there a reason she and Holland had to marry in secret?'

He shrugged. 'That her parents preferred a different husband?' Holland was an honourable knight, but Salisbury would be a landed Earl. Only a young foolish maiden, or an old fool like his father, would choose with the heart.

'So the Pope allowed the first man, Holland, to have the second marriage to Salisbury put aside and Lady Joan was restored to him.'

Nicholas nodded. 'Now, the Pope only wants to verify that all was done properly.'

In the silence, Islip drummed his fingers on the curved wooden arm of his cushioned chair. 'And the Earl of Salisbury has now married again,' he said, finally.

'I believe so.' What difference did it make?

'And so Thomas Holland's widow has once again entered into a clandestine marriage, but this time, with a man that, should she have deigned to ask, would have been forbidden.'

He should not have doubted the Archbishop's grasp of the situation. The man understood the complexities better than Nicholas himself. 'Yes. For two reasons, as I'm sure you recognise. They are too closely related because they share a grandfather. In addition, the Prince was godfather to one of her sons.' To stand as godfather to a child was to be as close as family.

'So once again, she ignores the laws of the Church,

and once again the Holy Father in Avignon blesses her actions. Now he comes to ask *me* if all is in order?'

Nicholas swallowed a smile and coughed. It was easy to understand the man's annoyance. He shared it. 'I believe what the Pope wanted was to create some inconvenience before bestowing his final blessing.'

'Well, he has done that,' Islip snapped. 'I wish he had been content to inconvenience the two people at fault. Or even someone who had a hand in the business. I was not even Archbishop then.'

'Who was?' It was not a fact that a fighting man had much use for.

'John de Stratford,' Islip answered. 'No man has more integrity. He even defied the King for the rights of the clergy.'

A strange statement. Did Islip have suspicions he did not share? 'I never suggested otherwise.'

'And he also chaired the King's council when Edward was on the other side of the Channel.'

All no doubt interesting to Islip, but not to Nicholas. So the Archbishop and the King had a complex relationship. That was true whenever the head of the state and the head of the church had to work together. 'All that is needed is to find the charter,' he said, trying to bring the man's attention back to the matter.

'All? That was three Archbishops ago. How am I to find the records now? What if they are gone?'

'What do you mean gone?' Couldn't the parchment pushers keep track of documents? 'One doesn't just misplace a communication with the Pope,' he snapped back. 'Particularly when it involves something like this. Someone must remember. Who were his clerks? Do you know?'

'Yes,' he answered, slowly. 'I was among them.'

Nicholas was surprised, though perhaps he shouldn't have been. 'And did you work on this case?'

The answer came slowly. 'No.'

Not surprising. He certainly would have said so before now if he had. Or perhaps not. The Archbishop seemed to be having trouble remembering, as the Prince had feared. Or, perhaps, his memory was selective.

'The records must still exist.' Dusty parchment, as the Prince had said. 'Someone must have copied the petition before it went.'

'To find them will take time.'

'Then you had best begin,' Nicholas snapped, tired of the tedium and heedless of his immortal soul. 'Time is the one thing we do not have.'

He bowed just low enough for ceremony, a request for the Archbishop to wave his hand and mutter a blessing so Nicholas had leave to go, but the man did not oblige. Finally, Nicholas raised his head. Islip sat, silent, eyes narrowed as if trying to peer into the past.

'More than ten years,' the man said, just above a whisper. 'Since then, we have lost a third of our people to the Death. And then more to the French. Who alive remembers where a single piece of parchment might be?' He looked at Nicholas, suddenly realising he was not alone. 'What if we cannot find it?'

Until they are wed, your task is undone. Dread

settled on his shoulder. What choices would be open to him then?

He met the man's eyes, to be certain he would be understood. 'If you cannot find it, then you will have the honour of informing His Grace and the Prince that they must cancel the wedding.'

All morning, Agatha had chattered away as Anne sat near a window in the common room, alternately looking down at her needle and up toward the street, watching for Nicholas's return.

The lodgings he had selected for them were within sight of the Cathedral, but designed for travellers, not pilgrims. No one minded that she stitched instead of prayed as she waited.

Though she did pray, silently and fervently, that Nicholas would discover nothing to raise his doubts.

That all would be as it must.

Yet when he walked in, a scowl marring his face, she bit her lip and motioned for Agatha to leave them. She saw no hint of suspicion, no reason to fear danger, and yet...

'You do not look pleased,' she said.

His eyes met hers and he seemed to soften, just for a moment. Because of her? She dared not hope for that.

He sank onto the tavern bench and called for ale. 'I've spent the morning trying to make a stubborn man of seventy remember and hurry. It went about as well as you would expect.'

She let a smile escape. No reason to fear. Yet. 'But all will be as it must.' Her voice held a question.

'You mean, as Edward and Joan want it?'

'As I do. And as you do, as well.'

He sighed. 'Yes, it will. He'll find what he needs to bless the previous dissolution or he'll bless their union without it.'

The tightness in her stomach eased. The scowl was impatience only. There was nothing to fear.

'I know it is not an easy thing and I thank you for that,' she said. 'I know Edward and Joan will, too.'

'Speak of other things,' he said, abruptly. 'What did you do today?' Today. She had waited by the window, as unmoving as a stone.

'I skipped about Canterbury's outer wall, then danced in a ring with the pilgrims waiting at the church's door.'

Shock appeared on his face at her words. They were bitter words she would never have used around Joan. But she had let resentment steal her tongue. What could she do? Nothing without help. Instead, she had thought of all she wanted to do, to have, to be. Things she would never have, no more than she would be able to skip or dance.

He shook his head. 'A thoughtless question.'

'A rude answer. What I did in truth was finish a piece of needlework that will be part of the hangings in my lady's new bedchamber.' She held it up, at once proud of the lush, green stitches and wistful that it would grace a marital bed.

He nodded, without really looking at it. 'Don't feel as if you have to say only what would please me.'

She smiled. 'It must be evident that I don't.'

'And you have heard me say things that...'

'That you are glad I have not shared with my lady?'

The ease of his smile warmed her. 'We have both, I think, had many years of minding our words.'

Oh, yes. Years and more until she had thought she would never, never be able to share herself with anyone. Even now, to reveal even a sliver of all she hid from the world day after day was a gift beyond measure, so precious that she could almost forget that earning his trust had been a duty to her lady.

'And I'm afraid,' he said, not waiting for her to answer, 'that I let my temper slip in front of the Archbishop today. But I knew little more than he did about the events surrounding Lady Joan's first dispensation from the Pope.'

She murmured something intended to sound sympathetic. Outside, the Cathedral's bells sounded, sparing her the need to speak in the silence that followed.

His gaze returned to her, as if he had discovered an idea. 'Do you?'

She was silent for too long.

'*Do* you, Anne?'

She rushed into speech, so she would not have to answer the question. 'What about the man who carried the petition to the Pope as you just did? That man would know something.'

'Who even remembers that man?' A foolish question,

but it seemed as if he were saying *who will remember me?* 'Do you know who he was?'

Safe to answer, since she did not. She shook her head.

She could almost see his thoughts as he explored other possibilities, other paths. 'But there must be someone. Who wrote the documents that were sent? Who talked to Lady Joan and Sir Thomas?'

She wanted to help him. No, to help her lady. To put all this quickly aside. 'I was but a child.' Only half the truth. She was twelve by then. She was as old as Joan had been when she and Holland first....

An impossible, sceptical frown now. 'Anne, it would help me, it would help your lady, if you could tell me anything else about all this. Obviously the Pope granted the petition, with the full support of the King and Queen. I know all was in order, I just need to find the pieces and put them together. The Prince said you have been with her for many years. Do you remember when Holland returned? Do you remember anything about that time?'

'I...' She swallowed. 'I was not in the household during most of it. I was with my lady.'

Surprise on his face. 'And where was she?'

'In the tower.'

Some combination of shock, confusion and comprehension mingled in his expression. 'What do you mean?'

'Salisbury...locked her there.'

'His own wife?'

'Or was she the wife of Thomas Holland?' Salisbury's wife, yes, who now wanted to leave him, now that the strong warrior Holland had come back into her life. But Salisbury was young, knighted less than a year, still foolish and hot-headed. He thought if he kept her away from Holland, she'd forget the man.

As she had once before.

'So did her counsel visit her there? To take her statement so he could represent her before the Pope?'

She shook her head. 'Salisbury would not allow it. She was kept under guard…' The memory of that year made her shudder. She had been her lady's sole companion for months. It had nearly driven them both mad.

'But the church requires that she testify, have counsel…'

She shrugged. She had said too much already. And she knew little of what had gone on beyond the tower walls while they waited together.

'How long?' His question, sharp. 'How long did this go on?'

The time had seemed endless then. 'I don't remember. A year?'

'But Salisbury let her speak, finally.'

'Yes.' She should have said nothing at all. To answer even one question would lead to more, to all the ones she must not answer.

'Why? Did the Archbishop intervene? Or the King?'

To answer would tell him too much. The King, the Queen, Joan's mother, all of them had supported Salisbury. But Holland, relentless, sent another plea to the Pope, and another and another… 'Such matters are beyond the knowledge of a maiden.'

She must end this. Now.

So she pushed herself to her feet and Nicholas immediately rose, reaching out to steady her, and she at once craved and feared to have him so near again. Now she was beginning to understand the hunger that drew Edward and Joan, the hunger that ignored everything that stood between them, the hunger that meant they would do anything, *anything,* to be together.

'And so, Sir Nicholas, I have reached Canterbury. While the Archbishop searches his files and his memory, may I visit the tomb of St Thomas?'

He nodded. 'Yes. You will have your pilgrimage, Anne.'

The hopeless, dishonest pilgrimage that she did not want.

Chapter Ten

The road leading to the Cathedral stretched before them, lined with pilgrims. Very few walked. The rest crawled, hobbled, crept forward on their knees. It was as if the very ground moved.

Hoping. Every one of them hoping for a miracle.

Anne did not hope.

Nicholas, beside her, touched her arm, his support stronger than the crutch that held her upright. He nodded to the road ahead. 'Do you want to…?'

'Crawl?' To get on hands and knees like a dog? Not in front of Nicholas. Not in front of anyone. 'No. God allows me the grace to stand upright. I shall keep my head high.'

He lifted his arms, as if uncertain whether she needed, or wanted, his help. 'What can I do?'

His question humbled her. Had anyone ever asked that of her? In that way? Not as if she must be pitied or hidden, but as if her wishes deserved to be honoured and her pain witnessed.

'I would be grateful,' she said, her voice as unsteady as her feet, 'if you would walk beside me.'

He nodded. 'I am no pilgrim, but I will see that you reach the shrine.'

Not because he cared, she told herself. Only because he was a man accustomed to making arrangements and solving problems. Still....

Together, they turned to the Cathedral. With Nicholas beside her she would approach the church door as if to seek blessing for a marriage.

Something she must never think.

A fraud, all of it. A pretence for her to be here at all. A diversion for today so he would ask no more questions, discover no more truths. Yet now that the great Cathedral rose before her, now that she forced herself to go through motions as if she were in a mystery play, it felt real. More real, more important than anything she had ever done.

And despite her refusal to hope, hope lifted her. Each step grew easier and gradually, the Cathedral loomed larger, as if it were a plant, growing taller before her eyes as it stretched toward the sun.

They walked not in respectful silence, but surrounded by noise—wailing, cries of pain, muttered prayers, and songs, songs that pilgrims sang so they would forget the miles passing beneath their feet.

And standing beside the road, even hawkers of souvenirs were yelling as if they were selling sweets in the market. 'Badges! Take home a badge!' The toothless pedlar waved a small, stamped tin emblem, the head of St Thomas Becket, wearing the mitre of his bishop's office, all framed by finely made arches that must have been copied from the Cathedral itself.

Nicholas paused. 'Let me buy one for you.'

'Look,' the man said, pulling out every sample of his wares. 'I have the saint in a ship and this one here shows the tomb itself, with all the detail. You see? That's beautiful work. And in this one they are killing the martyr, cutting off his head right in front of the altar.'

'Which one do you like?' Nicholas asked.

And suddenly, she *wanted* one, wanted something of her own that she could hold and look at and remember. *One day, a handsome man stood by my side and cared what I thought.*

The badge seller had laid out his collection on his left arm, marching up his sleeve from wrist to elbow.

She studied the riches, then pointed to St Thomas on horseback. 'That one.'

'To remind you that you rode all the way here.'

So quickly, he had understood. For some pilgrims, walking was penance, but she had conquered riding long distances.

'Thank you.' Hard words to say. She was weary of a lifetime of endless thanks. But she saw no pity in his eyes, no disdain in his gift.

He pulled out coin enough for two and took them both. Surprised, she watched him put one in his pouch and hand the other to her. It was unexpectedly light in her hand. 'Are you a pilgrim, too?'

'No,' he said, as they moved on. 'Yet I have travelled so many places and have carried nothing away from any of them. This time, I will have a memory.'

A memory. Was it of her? Or was it Canterbury that moved him?

She slipped the image of St Thomas into her pocket. Ahead of them, the line stretched, slow moving, to the Cathedral door, where a monk stood repeating the story of the martyred St Thomas to each pilgrim who entered.

It would be sunset, or dark, by the time she reached the shrine.

They moved slowly, without speaking, for some time. Then, she looked over at Nicholas, who seemed to be searching for another entrance, or an exit. Restless. Ready to move on.

'You need not stay with me,' she said. She had not expected him to come at all.

And when he looked at her, she could see she had caught him thinking of escape. 'I will not leave you. Not after you have come so far.'

Now she was the one ashamed, for she had not come for this, but at her lady's behest, sent to work a miracle of her own. A miracle to prevent Nicholas from finding out the truth, while he had been sent here at his lord's command, and that of the Pope, to do near the opposite.

She wondered which side God favoured.

'I do not want to make you wait,' she said. That, at least, was true.

'It is the Archbishop who is making me wait, not you. We can tell each other stories.'

A strange suggestion. She knew no stories.

'Unless you prefer to pray,' he said, quickly, when he saw the puzzled expression on her face.

Poor man, ever stumbling as if her lameness was his fault.

'No,' she said. No need for more prayers and supplication. Better to dream of the impossible than to remind God of her sins. 'Tell me of the places you have travelled. Tell me of France.'

France? Nicholas searched his memories. What was there to say of France?

He shrugged. 'All earth looks alike to a man at war, except where the marsh makes the land treacherous or the hills offer the best defence for battle.'

She looked at him as if he were jesting. 'You must have seen rivers, castles, cathedrals…'

They reached the stairs, he helped her climb and they paused by the monotone monk who told them the story they already knew. Then, they were shuffled to the transept where Becket had been killed. Wide-eyed, Anne seemed to gobble each vision, raising her eyes to the ceiling of the soaring Cathedral.

'Look.' She pointed to the coloured-glass windows. 'It looks as if God himself might live so high, then just reach out and create such beauty.'

He followed where her finger pointed, surprised at the excitement in her voice. She was a woman who had seemed to be awed by little. And yet this Cathedral…

He had not been a man to spend more time in

church than custom required. 'Yes, I saw cathedrals in France.'

And nowhere had he picked up so much as a rock. Yet here, he had paid for a badge. The man who had never wanted to be burdened with anything had chosen a cheap tin badge to carry away as a memento. To remind him of a saint?

Or was it Anne he wanted to remember?

'What cathedrals?' she said. 'Tell me? Did you see Chartres?'

Chartres. Yes, he knew that name. As he recalled, he had seen Chartres right after the terrible storm when the King decided to sign a treaty. Nicholas had been searching for benches and a scribe and the church was where he found them. 'Yes. I did.'

'What was it like? Was it as beautiful as this?'

He was grateful that she gazed back at Canterbury's windows and did not see him struggle to summon a vision of a church.

Any church.

But all that he remembered were dead men and exhausted horses and an unending cycle of light and dark. He had travelled countless miles through France and could remember nothing but the war that travelled with him.

She looked back at him, expectant. 'Or Notre Dame?'

The mirror of his memory was empty. 'I was not there to look at churches.'

Her smile drooped. 'What about castles? Mountains? The sea?'

He shook his head, feeling as if he had failed her.

But she washed the disappointment from her face. 'Then I will tell you of my travels. When I was in France with Lady Joan, we lived in a castle in Normandy with two round towers and a square tower. There was an abbey close by and at the top of one of the pillars was a carving of the Green Man with a great swoosh that made it look as if he was swallowing his own, long hair.'

She laughed at the memory and went on to describe the abbey's windows and the view from the castle's tower in such detail that he could see it before him. A castle he had visited, at least, he must have, but he could summon no more of it than that the curved walls looked strong, but should have been higher.

Yes, he had been there. And to so many other places, but he had focused only on the needs of the moment because he cared more to keep moving than to be where he was. There would always be some place new.

But Anne, forced to move slowly, all but trapped in each place, had absorbed the vision of it as if it were a gem, to be savoured and saved, treasured and revisited in memory in later days.

The loss of all he had seen, yet not *seen,* cut his breath. How many days, how many sights, had been lost to him? When he turned to look at the years behind him, he saw only war and mud and windswept sky.

Now, he was in England's most revered cathedral.

Today, he could take away more than a badge. He could take away a memory, a vision to summon up when he was days and miles gone from here. Something to remember of his life.

He looked around, but all he saw was a blur of pilgrims, all he heard was the din of their prayers and the monk's description of how the evil men cut off the head of the saint.

And in front of him, Anne smiled, silent, because she had realised he was no longer listening to her description of the abbey.

'How do you do it?' he asked.

'Do what?'

'How do you see so clearly, remember so much?'

They were close to Trinity Chapel now, and the tomb of the saint himself, crowded with pilgrims. 'Tell me what you see,' she said. 'Right now. Look down.'

'Stone.' Something to stand on. Something to walk over.

'Not just stone. See, this is older, more worn. And over there, it is newer. More polished.'

They had reached the stairs and she leaned on him to climb. One, two, three, four. Not quite in the chapel yet, but above the heads of the crowd, he could see the edge of the golden shrine, beckoning them. But instead of studying the tomb, he scanned the crowd, looking for a path of escape. There were so many people, so closely packed, that he could not see beyond them. What if he needed to get her away? How would he do that?

Beside him, a little breathless, she looked up at the windows and the carved pillars, as if she had come to see the Cathedral instead of to seek a cure. 'There, that window. It shows St Thomas's martyrdom. And the three murderers. And there, that one shows him curing the lame daughters of Godhold of Boxley.'

A moment before, he had thought only of how they would move through this space and how he would take care of her. Now, as he saw with her eyes, bits of colour became a story.

And he was struck with an unexpected sense of wonder. Not for the saint and his miracles, but for the men who had made such lasting beauty.

'How long have they been here?' he asked. 'These windows?'

She shook her head. 'I don't know. Hundreds of years.'

Hundreds. He had spent his life foolishly proud that he could arrange for food and supplies that would vanish within a day, handling details that would be forgotten by Yuletide. Meanwhile, with their lives, these nameless, long-dead men had left something that would last until the Second Coming.

What would he have at the end of it all? Nothing more than he had today. No home, no family, not even memories.

Nothing but a blur of days and miles, travelled, but not lived.

Relieved, Anne saw they had reached the final steps. Had Nicholas heard anything she had said?

Noticed anything around them? It did not matter now. Just a few more and she would be in the chapel with St Thomas's relics.

Steps again. One, two, three…an endless struggle. A good reminder. Struggle was her life, not this moment of joy. Not this strong arm offered to support her.

She let go of Nicholas. 'I will go on alone.'

He frowned. 'Are you certain?'

She nodded and turned her back on him.

Yes, she was certain. She had become weak and soft these last few days. Oh, the travel, the riding had been difficult, but she had been able to lean against this man, even dreaming that he might see more than the leg she dragged behind her.

More fool she. Not only could Nicholas threaten everything, but in a few weeks he would be gone.

She took each step carefully, no longer letting the windows distract her. Some of those around her could move no more easily than she. That was what she must remember. She was fortunate for only one reason. A reason she must not jeopardise.

Another step. Step seven, eight, almost done. The steps were as uneven as waves, worn by the feet of too many pilgrims to count. There were too many surrounding her now, a crush of broken humanity, some with wounds visible, others atoning for sins she could not see.

Now, close to their final goal, they began to push and shove. Someone knocked against her. Her stick slipped off the smooth worn stone and she went down on one knee, hard enough to rattle her teeth and make her bite her tongue.

No tears. No tears.

Her stick clattered down the stairs behind her and disappeared in the crowd, just as Nicholas had.

Do you want to crawl? It seemed as if God would insist on that. A good reminder. Penance for the lie that brought her here.

She tried to rise, but her bruised knee protested. Someone crawled over her hand. Her fingers slipped on stones worn as slick as ice, and she slid down a step.

Where was Nicholas?

But she saw only a wall of bodies between her and the tomb. Above their heads, the top of it shone like a golden sun embedded with twinkling rubies, so close it seemed that God must want her to reach it. Instead, she was going to slide to the bottom of the stairs and be trodden on by the next wave of seekers.

No more than she deserved…

Again, she stretched out her hand. Again, her fingers slid on the slick stone…

And then, she was lifted up, off the stairs, into his arms.

The last few steps, the steps she had struggled to mount, dissolved beneath his feet and suddenly, she was at the top, standing, her stick tucked firmly under her arm once more.

She clutched his sleeve. 'I did not realise, when I asked, how much I would need you,' she whispered. More than she wanted to.

'I will not leave you.'

'I know you did not intend…'

He shrugged and squeezed her hand before stepping behind her. 'We are all pilgrims now.'

No time to look around, to study, to remember. Pilgrims at the front fell to their knees. She joined them. Here, too, the stone had yielded to the years of knees. A groove worn by prayer…

The priest started to pray.

She could barely listen. This journey had been a sham, a pretence, an elaborate deception so that she could stay close to Nicholas as her lady had demanded. Why should God help her? She was a living lie. She had used the pilgrimage as a disguise instead of a pious act. There could be no miracle for Anne.

God had decreed her fate years ago.

Yet, as the words swirled over her head, something else surrounded her. Incense. Dizziness. The spirit of the saint himself, his earthly remains here, in front of her. Would it be possible…truly?

And suddenly, all the pretence, the falsehoods, fell away and there was only hope.

The priest stopped before her and held out an empty palm. She handed him the coin that Lady Joan had given her. Then he held the small vial, filled with the holy water of the saint for her to taste.

She wet her lips. Wanted more. Touched his hand and tried to drink.

He snatched it back and pressed his hand on her

head to keep it bowed. 'A drop is enough, if the saint chooses to help you.'

If the saint chooses...

Would he?

All she had to do was lift her leg and take a step.

Chapter Eleven

Prayers, unceasing, surrounded him, but Nicholas kept his gaze on Anne. Someone cried out, but he did not look to see who, or to wonder whether they shouted in joy or pain.

She knelt, still, the monk's palm cupping the curve of her head. And he prayed that God might grant her a miracle.

The monk moved on. She lifted her head.

Then, pushing herself up with her good left leg, and the crutch tucked under her right arm, she stood. For a moment, she was still, then she swayed, unsteady.

From his vantage point at the edge of the crowd, Nicholas held his breath as she lifted her lame right leg, pulling up the knee as if ready to step on that poor, useless foot.

She wobbled and he held his breath, holding her with his eyes as if his will alone could lift her to her feet and send her skipping down the stairs toward him.

She shifted her weight, as if she expected the leg to hold her...

And crumpled to the floor.

Before he could reach her, the rest of the pilgrims surged away from the tomb and down the stairs, washing around him like an ebbing wave. He battled his way up, pushing past a monk with an outstretched hand.

Below the glittering shrine that towered over them like a golden coffin, Anne lay silent and unmoving. He crouched beside her, tucked one arm beneath her knees, the other behind her back, and rose, carrying her down the treacherous stairs, away from the traitorous saint who had crushed her hopes.

And like an incoming wave, the next rush of pilgrims came up the stairs.

When Anne finally turned her eyes to his, the tremulous hope was gone, replaced by the familiar flatness of resignation.

'You can put me down,' she said, words devoid of life. 'It is over.'

A moment ago, she had sagged with weariness. Now, as if her spine was a sword, she was Anne again, refusing all pity.

Reluctantly, he put her on her feet and stayed close through the long journey through the nave. This time, she did not lift her head to study the stained glass crowning the door, but kept her eyes on the ground, as if each step must be watched.

Nicholas kept a hand near her waist as they navigated the streets between the Cathedral and the inn, slowly and silently. Her limp was even more pronounced than usual, now that the hope that had kept her upright was gone.

And his vaunted control was as shaky as her legs. All his proud detachment had disappeared. Now, not even his loins held sway. That would have been bad enough.

This was worse. Now his heart was in charge, the most dangerous of organs.

In sight of the inn, she stopped. 'Can we go somewhere else?'

'Yes, of course.' Where would she want to go? How could he relieve her mind of the saint's failure? 'There are other cathedrals.'

'I want nothing of churches.'

He cleared his throat and looked around. What was Canterbury but churches and pilgrims and reminders that her miracle had not come to pass?

I skipped about Canterbury's outer wall, she had said. Well, she might not skip, but he would find a way to lift her above it all.

'Come.'

Haltingly, but without question, she did, as they followed the street, crossed the bridge over the river and reached the West Gate. Many of the stones, placed there by the Romans, were missing now. He had been prepared to argue with the guard, but with the end of the war with France, the city fathers must have decided there were better uses for their funds. The door was open. The stairway, empty.

She took a deep breath, and started to climb.

'Anne, let me—'

'No.' She stopped him with a glance, stubborn and immovable. 'You will not be here to help me next time.'

And he bit back a response, knowing she was right. Behind her, he chafed at her slow progress, knowing he could have reached the top and returned before she completed the climb.

But when they reached the top and she drew a breath of air, he wanted to cheer with a strange sense of pride. She turned her back on the city and looked west, where streaks of orange clouds signalled the day's end. 'Is London in this direction?'

He nodded. 'And Windsor beyond.'

She turned to her left. 'And there? What lies over there?'

He assessed the sun. 'Dover. The Channel.' France. Spain. Italy.

She swung her arm in the other direction. 'And that way?' It was a game to her, pointing to all the places she would never see without her lady's leave. 'What would I find?'

He tried to remember the lay of the land. 'More water.' A day's travel, or less, to the north, south, and east. Close enough that he could smell the temptation of salt air. 'Almost any direction except to the west.'

He leaned against the wall next to her and looked back over the city. The Cathedral, inescapable, rose before him. 'You can see the towers clearly from here.' He tested his eyes, trying to capture a memory. The stone glowed copper in the reflected light of the sun. Yes, that he would remember.

Anne, looking away from the town, refused to turn.

Even though they were only a few feet above the street, the city looked different from here. The people were smaller, less distinct, as if they were no different one from the other as they sought shelter at day's end. How could God, high as He was, tell them apart? Even the saints were far above the earth. What had made them think St Thomas might look down and notice Anne of Stamford on her knees, begging for his attention?

And when God and the saints did glance toward the earth, it seemed solely to rain destruction from the heavens. As it did that day in France...

'I do remember something,' he said, quietly. 'About France.'

She turned, lips parted expectantly. Her hair, burnished by the same light that touched the church, glowed with the gold of a noble coin. 'Tell me.'

He swallowed. Suddenly, he wanted to forget the story of war. He wanted to sweep Anne close and take her lips again.

'It is not a comforting story.' He should think of something else. Something to give her hope or laughter.

Yet her wide mouth curved into a smile. 'Even a sad memory can comfort.'

Could it? What would she remember of him, when he was gone?

'This one does not.'

'Tell me anyway.'

And because she asked, and because he had not spoken of it since it happened, he did. 'We had besieged Paris and held high ground. The French would not come out to fight, but neither would they accept our terms for a treaty. And our men were hungry.'

Hungry because he had failed. The good grain he had found for them was gone. He had planned new supply lines, ordered vegetables and salted fish, grain and wine, all to arrive via ship. And to ensure there would be food, even if all did not arrive as scheduled, those left at Honfleur were to forage the countryside and send the results to Edward's army.

But the ships foundered or were attacked. The raiders sent barely enough for the King to eat and nothing at all for the horses.

'What happened then?' she said, softly, as if she knew he remembered all too clearly now.

'We had to retreat. On Easter Sunday we had to slink away as if we were cowards. And we marched all into the next day until we saw the towers of Chartres in the distance across the open plain.'

He remembered, though he did not want to remember. That brief moment, a warm, April day, sharp towers pointing to heaven. They had escaped, they could regroup, they could fight again. And then...

'And then, the heavens opened up. Thunder. Rain. Mud. And then the wind snapped from spring to winter as we marched through it. And the rain became sleet and then hail...' Frozen balls of ice, hurtling toward earth as if God himself were aiming at them. 'And then the ground froze.'

Wagons sunk into mud that hardened around them. Tents, saddles, cooking pots were abandoned for there were neither wagons nor horses to carry them. A few supplies came, at last. Too little. Too late. Hungry men and horses hadn't enough strength to fight the cold.

And when it was over, the road was lined with the corpses of those he had been charged to feed.

He pulled his gaze away from the Cathedral and away from the past and met her eyes. 'That's what I remember of Chartres. Cathedral towers swathed in sleet, looming over a battlefield of frozen mud. We could have beaten the French, but in the end, God had decreed who would be their King. Or that is what the King decided.'

A furrow of confusion appeared between Anne's eyebrows. 'But we won. We took so many hostages. The French owe us millions of marks.'

He smiled, a response of habit. He wondered what the Prince had told Lady Joan, for that, of course, was what Lady Joan had told her. 'Yes, of course. We won. But Edward is still not King of France.'

'And you think he would be if his men had been fed?'

Did he? Did he take that much blame, or credit? Neither the Prince nor the King had ever said so and yet...

He wanted no such responsibility again.

'I think,' he said, standing straight and handing her the stick, 'that it is time to return to the inn.'

Anne had walked beside him slowly. Once she was again in her room she stretched out on the bed, under the covers, grateful to be alone.

Her own sorrow, and his, hovered in the air and despair rolled over her, holding her fast against the straw-filled bed. Her leg, angry with disappointment, ached more than usual, ached so much that she let her tears flow, though whether pain or hopelessness was the cause, she did not know.

Both, it was clear, would be her companions unto death.

The physicians had spoken of humours and blood-letting, and even, when as a child she had wept at night, of the poppy, but that would only separate her from the world with a hazy layer of silk. It would not change the fact that a twisted foot distorted the rest of the leg.

Sometimes, rubbing and stretching the tight knots helped.

Sometimes.

She reached down and pulled off her garter and her hose, hoping a firm touch would work tonight.

Her mother had done this, long ago, stretched her toes one from the other, applied pressure to the bottom of her feet, near every night when she was a child. Sometimes her foot worked better afterwards. She might be able to move her foot from side to side or wiggle her toes. Such small things. Things other children did without thinking.

Her father had never touched the foot. Her father had never touched her at all.

With her mother's death, when Anne was fifteen, the strong hands were gone. No one else rubbed or stretched or touched or even wanted to see her foot.

And she wanted no one to.

So late at night, when the rest had fallen asleep, she would bend her left leg at the knee, painful in itself, and rub her foot until her hand was tired and cramped. And then, on fortunate nights, she would sleep.

This was her life. Food, clothing, shelter, work, submission to her lady. And the solitary pain. All the result of an exchange her mother had made to protect her from a fate much worse.

She flexed her foot, biting her cheeks to fight the pain.

'Anne?' A knock on the door. Nicholas.

'Yes?'

'May I come in?'

She straightened her legs, smoothed her skirt over them, and pulled up the bedcovers. He must not see her foot, her leg. 'Yes. Come.' Blessedly, a woman's legs were easy to hide.

Men's were not, she was reminded, as Nicholas stepped into the room. His long legs, sporting blue hose and exposed by a short tunic, would have drawn her eye even if she had not been jealous of their strength.

'I should not have spoken of France,' he said. A blunt beginning.

'I should not have asked you to remember,' she said. Her pain was clearly evident. That of others was not. And if she wanted to keep her secrets, she must respect his.

He paced a few steps. 'Are you hungry? Do you need anything?'

She shook her head. Her foot was not the only part of her that must stay hidden. There was more, something even less visible.

The part that looked at him and lied.

Nicholas stepped to the edge of the bed, still berating himself for having disclosed things she did not need to know, particularly after she had just had her own hope snatched away. 'Are you…all right?' Not admitting, even to himself, that he, too, still hoped for a miracle.

'Again, you have done me a kindness. Not only today, but this…' She waved a hand at the room.

He had spent an outrageous sum to ensure she did not have to share her space this night. 'It is little enough.' His way of apologising for the saint's failures.

'I must thank you,' she said. Her chin was lifted as if she resented having to say the words. 'For helping me at the shrine.'

'I'm sorry,' he said, finally. Sorry for everything about her life that he could not help. Words he hated to say. It was his job never to have to say them. His job to make all the rough places smooth.

But even he could not fight God. That had been proven more than once.

'I don't want your pity.'

'And you'll not have it.' Was it her anger that gave her such strength, day after day? 'It's not pity I feel.'

'Then what would you call it?'

He didn't know. Or didn't want to. 'It does not need a name.' To name it would be dangerous. To name it would be to admit to exactly the weakness he had railed against all his life.

Silence swelled.

He should move. He should leave. She was well, or as well as she could be. There was no reason for him to stay.

Yet his feet remained rooted to the floor.

She sighed, finally, and waved a hand, inviting him to sit. He perched on the edge of the narrow bed and without thinking, he glanced down at her legs, hidden by sheets and skirt.

'No,' she said abruptly, her smile broken. 'There is no change. It is as it has always been.'

He knew that. 'But sometimes, the healing comes later.' So he'd been told. And so believed the hundreds of pilgrims who came and never left, waiting, hoping, that their cure would come.

'Do you seek to comfort me?'

'I thought, perhaps…' What had he thought? Attempting to give her hope, he had raised his own. He knew better. He knew that he must depend on himself, and not on God.

'Do not.' Sharp words. Carrying their own pain. 'Here. Look. There is no miracle.'

She pulled back the sheet.

There, just below the hem of her skirt, her crippled right foot lay exposed.

In truth, it was not as bad as he had imagined. Misshapen, but not monstrous. It looked for all the world like a baby's foot, toes curled, ankle twisted sharply to the side, so the sole of the foot could never feel the firmness of the earth.

He stretched out his fingers…

'Don't!' She shoved her feet out of sight beneath the rumpled linen and pulled the covers up. 'Are you satisfied?'

Yet he reached for her foot anyway, cupped his hand over the blanket that shielded it.

She held a palm on his cheek and turned his face to hers, forcing his gaze away from her foot. And her eyes clung to his, waiting for his verdict.

What could he say? To belittle it, to say it was only a twisted foot and not a monstrous growth would demean the suffering she had carried all her life.

'It has been with you,' he began, his hand resting lightly on her skirt, 'like this, all your life?'

She let out a breath and lifted her chin. 'Yes.'

'And yet, you work, you serve your lady, just as any woman might.'

She hesitated. 'Yes.' The word had a question in it, as if she did not know why he said so.

'Then,' he raised his eyes again, 'since it is part of who you are, I must also hold it dear.'

She gasped.

He cupped her head in his hands, lifted her face to his and kissed her.

Her lips moved over his, soft and gentle, and, surprisingly, so was the kiss. A kiss not of passion, but of dreams. Of tumbling slowly into something inevitable and irresistible, for good or ill, impossible to resist.

He did not stop to ask himself why he did this. Or why she did. If he let himself think, he, she, both of them might wake from the dream. And for once, that was not what he wanted.

They parted only for a breath before her lips took his again.

He had no thoughts after that. At least, none that found words.

Chapter Twelve

Anne's first thought was to fight, not surrender. She had struggled all her life against her feeble flesh, refusing to yield to its weakness, refusing to be the slave of pain. She could not ignore her damaged leg, but she could suffer it as a knight might suffer a scar of battle, knowing he had earned it bravely.

Pleasure was still an unfamiliar foe, yet even against pleasure, she might have triumphed. It was the heart's want that she could not fight. The want that he must not see. The want she had buried so deeply she no longer knew it was there, so when it rose, fierce and fiery as a dragon, she had no defence. She simply let herself be kissed.

And then, she kissed back.

She couldn't stop the gasp of desire that gripped her throat, the tears that burned her eyes at the realisation that someone would want to get so close. Without judgement. With desire.

At least one time.

One of them—he? She?—took a breath. A pause that broke the kiss only to let him take her lips again

But with that breath, she was Anne again. Anne with ugly hair and a lame foot and nothing but lies to tell this man.

She pursed her lips, pushed him away and squeezed her eyes shut so he would not see the wistful look that must have crept into her gaze. She should not have kissed him. Not the first time and not the second and least of all now.

Safer to remain ignored and unseen.

He stood and stepped away, out of reach, seeking distance as much as she, and parted his lips to speak.

'Don't!' she said. Her strength was gone. His regrets would only sharpen her own. 'Do not say you are sorry.'

'Sorry?'

She held her breath, waiting for him to break the silence.

'I am not sorry,' he said at last. 'I am not sorry at all.'

If he had crossed the room to touch her again, she would have turned to fire, a flame of yes and yes and yes once more.

But he did not. He left the room, pulling the wooden door behind him, and not until she could no longer hear his steps did she breathe.

He had not kissed her out of pity and he was not sorry that he had and that was the most frightening thing of all.

* * *

Nicholas slept little that night, so when the Archbishop summoned him to the Priory the next morning, he wasted little time.

As soon as he arrived, and without ceremony, the man thrust a parchment into his hands. 'Here.'

He glanced at the carefully written lines. He had a little Latin, more than most of his station, so he stumbled through, trying to decipher the words.

Silence stretched.

'It says,' the Archbishop said, finally, 'that given that Thomas Holland and Joan plighted their troth before a witness months prior to her marriage to Salisbury, the church says that marriage is valid, the marriage to Salisbury should be put aside and the Pope should so judge the same.'

All as he had expected. 'So it is confirmed,' he said, with a surprising sense of relief. 'You will rule accordingly.'

He had not realised until that moment that he had feared they might not find it at all.

'I will gather the bishops together. We will review the document—'

'Review? Is there something irregular?'

Islip frowned, the lines in his brow as deep as furrows cut by a plough. 'Let us hope, for all our sakes, that there was not.'

An odd comment. Nicholas shrugged off the worry. Nothing could be wrong. Lady Joan had been raised under the protection of the King and Queen. The stakes had been too high then.

They were even higher now.

'So if there is nothing irregular,' he began, 'how long will all this take?'

'How long before they can wed in truth, you mean?'

How long before I can leave this island? was what he actually meant, but Nicholas nodded. 'The official word from Avignon is expected soon after Michaelmas.' In less than two months.

'We will be done by then. I will send word directly to the King.' His face relaxed then. 'I look forward to celebrating the Prince's wedding ceremony.' As Primate of All England, the duty would fall to him. 'Will they marry at Windsor?'

'I believe so.' He shrugged, not caring. His work was done. He could return Anne to court and be free of all the responsibilities and complications of these last few weeks. The unwelcome feelings he had for her would fade, he was certain, as soon as he set foot on a ship.

He bowed respectful thanks and turned to go, but as he did, the Archbishop's summation of the document echoed in his head. The words had slipped by then, but thinking back, they clanged loud as a church bell.

...Holland and Joan plighted their troth before a witness...

He turned back to the Archbishop. 'It said vows were exchanged before a witness.'

'Yes.'

'Who? What is the name?'

Islip raised his brows. 'Do you think to question them?'

He had thought nothing of this at all until it became so difficult. 'That's not necessary, is it?'

'Let us hope not. It does not list a name.'

'Wouldn't it be customary? For the witness to be named?'

'It is not customary,' Islip said, his temper short again, 'for a clandestine wedding to be witnessed at all!'

Not customary at all. Yet in the midst of a foreign city and a war, a twelve-year-old maiden and a twenty-six-year-old man had been careful enough to find a witness who conveniently appeared and then disappeared. Who?

And why?

Anne sat in the inn's common room all morning, stitching another new emblem for the Prince's bed hangings, lifting her eyes occasionally to see today's hopeful pilgrims passing by on their way to the Cathedral.

Agatha had begged leave to go with Eustace and buy her own token of her visit to Canterbury and Anne had let her go. She suspected the maid's sudden desire for a pilgrim's badge had more to do with Nicholas's squire than with piety, but their absence relieved her of the need to talk.

Soon, Nicholas would return from his visit with the Archbishop. She could only pray he had received what he needed and that they could return to the court, where she knew what her life must be and what was expected of her and she could be invisible Anne again.

He had seen her and did not shame her or revile her or look at her with pity. He saw her and accepted, even respected what he saw. He saw Anne and not Anne's limp. When had anyone done that?

Her father had seen nothing but the limp, so he wanted not to see her at all.

Even her mother had seen her lameness first and arranged Anne's life around it, particularly after her father had died and left them with little. When she searched her memories of her mother, all she found were worries. Was Anne safe? Was Anne in pain? How would Anne live? The entire, elaborate web of secrets, all because she did not think Anne could make a life. Not because she was Anne.

Because she limped.

Anne was fortunate, she supposed, that she had not been drowned like a kitten or that people had not cursed her and her mother both for God's punishment, for there were those who still believed that such ills were retribution from God. Yet the pestilence had taken bishops and children, the evil and the good.

But until she met Nicholas, how long had it been since anyone had touched her? All these years, alone, since her mother's death. Years in which no one but Lady Joan would come close enough to risk brushing her skirt or her skin. She had donned invisible armour, strong enough to ward off any approach. Strong enough to make Anne herself disappear.

While Lady Joan, the most beautiful woman in the kingdom, floated through life on a sea of admiring glances, no one saw Anne. No lingering looks lifted her gracefully through the day. No knight, no page, not even the man who emptied the night waste had ever looked at her and smiled in delight at what he saw.

Until now.

Yes, people had averted their eyes. So had she. She did not want to look, to know the thing.

But this man, rife with his own buried pain, had seen that which was hidden, touched the untouchable, acknowledged what no one else would.

Dangerous. So dangerous to be so close to a man who really saw her, beyond the obvious, beyond her limp. There were things he must *not* see. Things that must be as hidden as her twisted foot.

Things that made Nicholas the most dangerous of all men.

Late in the afternoon, sun rays slanted in the window. She looked around to check the room was empty, then raised her skirt to look at her foot, safely hidden beneath red hose.

As Nicholas had said, sometimes the healing did not happen immediately. Sometimes, people waited near the healing shrine until they recovered. Or died.

Maybe—

At the sound of the door, she dropped her skirt, picked up her needle, and looked up to see Nicholas, scowling, at the inn's door.

'What's wrong?' she said, not waiting for a greeting. 'Didn't the Archbishop find the document?'

'He found it.'

'Did he find something wrong?' A question she should never have asked. Nothing could be wrong. Not after all these years.

'He did not. It will be summarily blessed by a gathering of bishops, purely for the sake of spectacle.'

'So all is well.'

He growled. 'For them, yes.'

'And for you?'

'There was a witness to that wedding.'

Her heart started pounding, as if a ghost had finally escaped the dungeon she had hoped would hold him for ever. 'How do you know that?' Her words were as shaky as her leg.

'It said so. In the petition.'

'Did it say who?'

'No.' He looked at her, then, as if seeing her as a link to all that had gone before. 'Do you know?'

'Why would I know?' She wanted to say she was sorry she must lie to him. 'I was no more than four.'

'But don't you find it strange? That a clandestine wedding should have a witness?'

She shook her head and looked down at her stitching, yet another copy of the emblem of the Prince of Wales. White feathers. The motto *Ich Dien*. I serve.

And that was what Anne would continue to do.

'Not so strange,' she said. A risk, now, but she must take it. She must steer him away from that wedding and back to this one. 'I witnessed her wedding to the Prince.'

He stared, as if struck dumb. 'What? Why?'

'Because she asked me to.'

Shock quickly merged with anger. 'And you didn't tell me?'

A shrug. As if it were of no significance. *Now meet his eyes, as if you have nothing to hide.* 'Is it important?' Last night's kiss still burned on her lips, lips she would use to tell him all about this wedding.

The one that didn't matter.

'That night, Lady Joan woke me and asked me to come with her. She did not say why. But when we entered the chapel, I saw the Prince and then—' another shrug '—they exchanged their vows.'

'You knew the marriage was forbidden.'

You mustn't. You cannot! The King, you are too close... 'The entire court knew that.'

'Then why didn't you stop them?'

Laughter came easily then. 'Am I to tell the Prince of Wales and the Countess of Kent what they cannot do?'

'But you knew what would happen, how grave the danger, to their souls, to the kingdom!'

'I did, but what I did not know is how deeply it would trouble Sir Nicholas Lovayne to be called on to resolve the issue.' He had barked at her as if he, not the kingdom, had been affronted.

'That is not what troubles me.' Hurried words. Angry.

And as his temper rose, hers must fall. 'Then why are you so angry?' Yet as she asked, she knew.

He stood and she could see him wrap himself in calm, as protective as a cloak. 'When next you witness their wedding, you will see one the church can bless,' he said, letting her question lie unanswered. 'We return to the court in the morning.'

She rose, eager to retreat to her room. 'I will be ready.' Ready to leave this man who had a habit of goading her to say too much.

Or perhaps it was her own weakness that made her say things she should not? How had she kept the secret all these years, she wondered, as she climbed the stairs to her room, when after a few days and a few kisses he had her babbling of things she should not?

Yet how could she have understood the freedom of being away from Lady Joan? All her life, in her lady's presence, she had rarely said more than yes, my lady, no, my lady, thank you, my lady, all the while bursting to say more.

Well, her confession had done what she had intended. It turned his attention to this wedding and away from the other one.

The one her mother had claimed to witness.

Nicholas spent the rest of the day concerning himself with details he could control: making sure the horses were ready, packing food for the journey. The court had returned to Windsor, which would cut the return trip down to scarcely five days.

Five days too many to spend with Anne of Stamford.

Why are you so angry?

He was still wrestling with her question the next morning, as he walked to the stables to retrieve his horse. The inn's stable had not had room for all their mounts and he wanted the time away from her, from Eustace and the others, just to think.

Anne had tweaked him with her suggestion that he resented the difficulty of unravelling the Prince's impulsive marriage. Six weeks travelling to Avignon, innumerable days arguing with papal clerks, then the same, long journey back, only to be handed one last task before he was finally free. Yes, he was irritated and impatient.

But that was not the reason for the visceral, unfamiliar fury that had moved him when he discovered that Anne had witnessed the wedding and never told him.

From the beginning, the woman had stirred unwelcome emotions—possession, tenderness, lust and now anger—all those crazed passions he had so proudly spent his life avoiding. The ones that drove men like his father and the Prince into the arms of women who, finally, held them as tight as a prison.

But when he was drawn to Anne, he let his head convince him that it was logical, or at least harmless, to pass the time with her. Meanwhile, he ignored the urges that originated below his neck.

In his loins.

Or even in his heart.

She had sparked feelings he did not even recognise. From hope and prayer for her to find her miracle

to a willingness to confess his own failures to a desire so strong that he nearly went far beyond a kiss.
A kiss that was still on his lips when she told him—

He stopped in mid-stride in the centre of Canterbury's busiest street as he realised the truth he should
have known all along.

He was angry because she had lied.

She had fooled him because he had started to believe she was different from other women. She wasn't.
She had created an illusion, lured him in, all the while
concealing anything she did not want him to know.

He had been no wiser than his father, trusting her,
thinking she trusted him, but if she had, she would
have shared such a confidence long before.

It made him wonder what else she hid.

Close to Lady Joan, yes. Closer than he had ever
imagined.

She had made it clear where her loyalty lay.

A good reminder of a lesson he thought long ago
ingrained. Never trust emotions, particularly when
it came to women.

As he mounted his horse, his girdle purse swung
against his thigh with a gentle thud. Gathering the
reins in his left hand, he reached inside, prinking his
finger on the edge of St Thomas's mitre.

The pilgrim badge.

He had broken his rule. Reached for a reminder.
Weighed himself down with a token of remembrance.

Nicholas turned the horse toward the inn and
bent his elbow, ready to hurl the bauble across the
muddy street.

At the last moment, he looked down and rubbed his finger over the sharp, pressed pewter and remembered.

The stubborn set of her jaw, refusing to allow either pain or pity to rule her. Her laughter. Her repudiation of fawning flattery or grovelling thanks when he reached out a hand to help her.

The press of her body against his. The soft hunger of her lips. The way she had forced him to *see*.

He rounded the corner to see the rest of them already gathered with the horses, waiting. Anne was studying the church across from the inn, no doubt memorising the number of stones.

No. He would collect no more memories. Each one, heavy as a stone, would weigh him down, hold him back. He would let go of this woman and move on to the life he planned.

He dropped his hand and let the medal fall to the dirt, to be trampled by the next passing horse.

He wanted no reminders of this journey.

Chapter Thirteen

The gate of Windsor Castle rose before him, a blessed end to a journey which had seemed longer than all the ones before. Other than to see that she was comfortable and safe, Nicholas had tried to stay away from Anne, but he had been forced to step in when the others kept tangling the straps he had designed to hold her firmly to her patient jennet.

He knew that avoidance was only the mirror of desire, both weaknesses of the heart. But as the miles unrolled behind them, he told himself a different story. She had withheld the truth deliberately. It was no sin of omission, no accident. And it had nothing to do with her trust of him.

She had concealed her part in the wedding for some other reason. Whatever that might be, it was reason enough for him to be suspicious.

But he wanted no more mysteries to unravel. The Archbishop and the Pope were appeased. All that was to be done was to have a redundant ceremony so the

Prince and his bride could be off to bed, Nicholas off
to France and Anne off to...

Well, he didn't care.

But now, even at Windsor's gates, carts of building stone stretched between here and the journey's
end, forcing him to ride around them to gain entrance.

Windsor itself he barely recognised. The new entrance with massive stone turrets had been completed
in the spring, before he left for France, along with
lodgings opposite the chapel, where he would, no
doubt, find a bed. In the months he had been away,
it seemed that the French peace payments had transformed into men and stone.

Workmen swarmed the castle grounds. Blocks of
white, brown and green stone littered the yard, along
with stacks of wood. The smell of the iron worker's
charcoal hung in the air. Strong walls, looking more
like a church than a fortress, were rising on the north
side of the upper bailey.

Sparing a moment's sympathy for the man taking charge of it all, he swung out of the saddle and
handed the reins to Eustace. He was done with all
that, he reminded himself, as he went to help Anne
off her horse for the last time.

'Thank you,' she said, then rested her fingers on
the leather straps that had held her steady for the days
and miles past. 'May I keep it?'

He waved a hand in agreement. What use did he
have for a leather harness designed for her comfort?

'Will I see you again?' she asked, as Agatha called
over a servant to unload their horses.

'I don't think so.' If God had been merciful, the ransom for his hostage would be waiting for him, money enough for him to buy the second warhorse he needed, some arms for Eustace, and then book passage to France. From there, he would find the Great Company, and lose himself in the fighting. 'I'll leave as soon as I can.'

'Then God keep you safe on your journey.' She took a deep breath and let it go, as if she were letting him go, as well, and then turned to confer with Agatha about what rooms would be theirs.

The King and Queen had not yet returned to Windsor, but Edward and Joan had moved their households here to begin planning for the expected wedding. Until the new palace was finished, the royal family was housed in the round tower perched on a hill in the centre of the Windsor grounds.

Nicholas turned to the tower, but the Prince had not waited for him to be officially announced; he had rather appeared beside him, out of breath as if he had run all the way.

Hope and worry met in his eyes. 'Well?'

'Yes.' Nicholas had the sudden urge to put his arm around Edward's shoulder in reassurance. 'All is well.'

The Prince roared in delight and sent servants scurrying to find wine and the Lady Joan as they mounted the stairs back to Edward's rooms in the tower.

So easy for two fighting men, he thought, as they

left the keep behind them. So difficult for Anne, who would struggle with stick and stair.

He looked behind him, hoping he would not see her on her knees again, but Edward would not let him pause until they reached his rooms and red wine filled their silver goblets.

'To Sir Nicholas Lovayne,' Edward said, lifting the cup. 'Who has made it possible for me to reach heaven on earth.'

Nicholas's pride, usually hidden, broke into a smile. No, he might not have noticed the coloured windows of Canterbury's Cathedral, but he had served his sovereign and the Prince as well, or better, than any man could have. 'How soon?' the Prince asked. 'When can we wed again?'

'A few weeks. No more.'

Edward's smile dimmed. 'So long? I cannot wait to have my bride back in my bed.'

A bold statement about a future Queen, Nicholas thought, though he suspected she shared the sentiment. Weak fools, both of them, to be driven by such want. An unwelcome reminder of his own weakness.

What had Anne called it?

Bliss. But what man, even a Prince, was given heaven on earth?

'No more than two months,' he said. But long enough. By then, if he were fortunate, he would be across the Channel and have joined forces with the company of mercenaries, doing exactly what he longed to do. 'Did the ransom arrive?'

'No,' Edward said, wiping his wine-soaked moustache on his sleeve. 'And so, my friend, you cannot leave me yet. You must witness the wedding you made possible. But you will receive something from me. Small enough thanks for my happiness.'

The sum he named was generous. It would keep his hostage fed and his gaoler paid until the payment came from France.

'And so, my friend, until then, enjoy the hunt, the gaming and even a diversion with the ladies.'

There was only one lady that came to his mind. The very one he wanted to forget.

The Prince called for his hunt master, already turning his attention away from the wedding and all the difficulties Nicholas had conquered to make it possible.

It was done. Finished. His work complete.

So why did he still wonder?

'Edward, was there someone else there that night?'

The Prince was listening with half an ear. 'What night?'

'When you and Joan wed?'

A sudden look. He had the man's attention. 'Why?'

He shook his head. 'Anne said that she had been there.'

'To the wedding? Does it matter?' The question, direct as a hawk, hung in the air.

'No.' It made no difference at all. Not to anything or anyone but Nicholas. 'I was just…surprised.'

'If it does not matter, do not think of it again.' The Prince's smile returned. 'She was there, I guess. I saw only Joan.'

'Why did Lady Joan bring her?'

'She said we should have a witness. That a witness would be important.'

It had been important to one of Joan's weddings. But not to this one. Not to her wedding to the Prince. 'It isn't necessary,' Nicholas said, taking a sip of wine, the silver cup cold on his lips. 'It is not even customary.'

'Well, who knows why a woman does anything? A fantasy of hers, perhaps. Women love to chatter. She and the girl are close.'

Close, yes, but not equals. Joan would share no confidences with Anne. Or would she?

Had she?

Or was he acting no more logically than a child, snubbed at play?

Nicholas set the cup on the table and ran his finger idly around the rim instead of looking at the Prince to signal that his question was equally idle. 'There was a witness at Lady Joan's first clandestine marriage. The one to Holland.' Now he would look. 'Did you know that?'

'I did not know. Neither do I care.' His jolly humour had soured at the mention of another husband. 'The only wedding of Joan's that interests me is the one that joins her to me'

'Lady Joan would remember. Maybe I'll ask her.'

'You will not.' The Prince drained his cup and slammed it on the table. 'I want her thinking of our wedding. Not any other. Don't make a river of a raindrop.'

Was he? What difference did it make now? It was only an absent detail, nothing more. And he had let himself growl over it as if he were a hungry dog, upsetting the Prince in the process.

He smiled. 'You're right. I'm accustomed to having the steer of every situation.' Including his feelings. Instead, he had pouted like a grumpy child, deprived of a sweet. Anne must have thought him mad.

'A good hunt will clear your head,' the Prince said. 'I will wager you that I get the first kill.'

He needed something more than that. He needed to prove he could speak to Anne of Stamford without foolish feelings getting in the way. And he would. Eventually.

Both Anne and the Prince had reassured Lady Joan that all was well, so, after a brief expression of disappointment in St Thomas for his failure to deliver a miracle, the bride-to-be plunged into wedding preparations, which began the next morning with a discussion of music.

'I would prefer,' Lady Joan began, 'to have the Queen's minstrels play at the feast.'

'Not Edward's?' The Prince, the King and the Queen each had their own musicians. 'Or the King's?' Anne was fond of the music of the King's trumpeters and drummers. It made her feel strong.

'They are good, of course.' Apologising, as if her preference might insult one of the Edwards, even though neither was within earshot. 'The King's harp player I like very much. But the others' music is more…'

She sighed. 'It sounds as if they are playing for men going to battle.'

Anne refrained from stating that that was, of course, one of their primary jobs. She wondered whether Nicholas had been forced to worry about dented trumpets on the battlefield.

She wondered why she was still thinking of him.

She had begun, foolishly, to dream, if not to hope. He had been kind. More kind than anyone she had known. More than kind when she remembered the kiss…

I'm not sorry.

No. A man would never be sorry for taking a kiss. It meant nothing.

A lie. It had meant more than either of them wanted it to mean. It meant even more that her confession had angered him. Meant so much that he had spent all the days since at a distance. And for that, strangely, she was grateful. She had already said too much. Another kiss, another touch, the two of them alone with a bed…

She would not have been able to resist.

All was behind her now. He was gone. Her life would be as it had always been.

All would be as it must.

A knock on the door. The court tailor and a cloth merchant scurried in. Bowing, the man started to spread out his wares.

'This silk from Italy would make a lovely wedding gown,' he began, pulling out a length as long as his arm. 'It would favour your eyes.'

Anne put down her work to gaze at the colour. Deeper blue than Lady Joan's eyes. Deeper even than the sky. More like the coloured glass of the cathedral. Yet blue signified purity. Not exactly the best reminder of Lady Joan's marital history.

She met her lady's glance and shook her head.

The merchant did not hesitate. 'Or here, the marbryn.'

Lady Joan dismissed it with a raised brow. 'Last Yuletide we wore that.'

He put the multi-coloured fabric aside. The Queen would be sorry. She had liked that one.

'Now this…' He pulled out a shimmering fabric.

Anne blinked. It was like looking at the sun sparkling on a necklace of gold.

'Yes,' her lady said. 'The cloth of gold. Have you enough for my gown and a mantle?'

The merchant closed his eyes and touched his fingers. Then he finished counting, he smiled. 'Forty ells, I think. Yes.'

'What about for surcoats for the minstrels?'

The man's eyes widened and he swallowed. 'How many minstrels, my lady?'

Agatha crept back into the room and handed Anne her scissors, a reminder of who, and what, she was.

'Were they not where I said?' Anne whispered, as the dressmaker and the cloth merchant conferred. She had sent the girl to retrieve them near an hour before.

Agatha looked down, a tinge of pink on her cheek. 'Yes.'

Anne recognised that look. 'Did something else delay you?'

'I just stopped for a moment. I thought he would be leaving.'

Oh, so did I, Anne thought. So did I. 'Eustace, you mean?'

She nodded, unable to contain a smile. 'But he's not. Not until the wedding is over.'

Anne opened her mouth to warn the girl. She must not hope for things she could not have. The squire would be a knight some day, far above a serving girl. In the end, she would have nothing but a wounded heart and a pilgrim badge.

Nothing more than Anne herself.

So she returned to her stitches. She was not qualified to lecture on a lesson she had not learned. Her heart, too, had leapt with joy to think that Nicholas would be here for another day, week, even a month or more. She could only hope their paths would not cross.

In fact, she would work to make certain they did not.

Nicholas was fortunate not to see Anne again for days. He needed time to think of the words, to steel himself to say a simple apology for being no more chivalrous than a boor.

And to convince himself the reason for his rudeness was nothing more than fatigue or the phase of the moon.

Even his speech to the King had not been rehearsed as carefully as this. He had said he was sorry to her, of course. But he had been sorry for what God, or life, or the world had done to her. Not for a regret of his own.

And then, once he had found the words, he must find the opportunity. A time and place where he would not be overheard. Where his *mea culpa* would be received by the only person who deserved to hear it.

In fact, it took several days before he could not only find the words, but the equilibrium with which to say them. Once he did, once he was ready and she did not appear, the resentment flickered again. She must be avoiding him. The thought was laughable, of course, and sent him on a new spiral of arguments with himself.

So when he finally saw her, it was not at all as he had planned.

He was as drunk as a sheep.

The Prince had embarked on a full round of celebrations and Nicholas had been toasted and fêted and honoured day after day. Late one evening, he found himself lost, trying to work his way through the timber-framed building Edward had tucked inside the ancient stone of the Round Tower, clutching a candle and searching for his bed and a garderobe.

But not in that order.

So when a woman with a crutch rose out of the

darkness before him, at first he thought he dreamt.
'Anne?' Would a vision in a dream answer?

'Nicholas?'

No dream, perhaps. He took another step and
tripped, sprawling across the floor.

The laughter—no, that was not what he would
dream. It was Anne.

He groped for the candle, but it had rolled away,
flame extinguished. Gingerly, he moved his legs, his
knee and hip as wounded as his pride.

In the dark, he could hear her catch her breath, trying to douse her mirth. 'I don't think I could lift you,'
she began, 'but I could lend you my crutch.'

And at that, he had to laugh, too. No way to main-
tain dignity or present himself as a rational, logical
man. No way to apologise in grave tones or explain
away a momentary pique. The man who fixed things,
solved problems, smoothed over all difficulties, could
not even rise from the floor unaided.

He sighed, his tongue loosened just enough by
the wine he had drunk. 'Ah, Anne. I had planned
to apologise for behaving rudely on the way home
from Canterbury, but you have just seen me at my
worst. Accept my total humiliation as a token of my
deep regret.'

Thankfully, she did not laugh again, but lowered
herself to the floor, relieving him of the need to struggle to his feet.

Sitting next to her, wrapped in darkness, felt as
private and intimate as in the confessional booth.

'I accept,' she whispered. 'But you must pay a penance.'

'Will the aching head I am sure to have in the morning not be penance enough?'

She must have shaken her head. 'I revealed something of myself and you spurned me for it. Your punishment shall be to answer my questions.'

So that you can scorn me? He had told her already of his greatest failure and she had said nothing, but she was a woman, and did not understand the demands of war. 'Ask.'

'First, where are you from?'

Where are you from?

Why did his lips freeze on the reply?

He could barely summon an image of the countryside of his childhood. A marsh. A meadow. All things he had left to forget.

'Lincolnshire. I was born in Lincolnshire.' He pushed himself up from the floor. If he were to deal with the past, he must at least be sitting upright.

'Is your family still there?'

Family. Did he have such a thing? His mother had died before he could remember. There was nothing for him in Lincolnshire. Not then, and certainly not now.

'My mother died. My father never left. He died two miles from the place he was born.'

Not in Scotland or France. Not serving his King with the proud English longbow as he had dreamed. Instead, he died a tanner, permeated with the stink of animal skins. Trapped by his lust into marrying a woman who had presented herself as a chaste maiden instead of an experienced wench, already with child.

Lust was not to be trusted, Nicholas had decided. Even his own.

'So you have no one?' There was surprise, concern in her voice.

'No.' No one he wanted to remember.

His stepmother had preferred her own son to him. And Nicholas had allowed his feelings to rule him. He had kicked, screamed, disappeared for hours. He wanted nothing of home, nor they of him.

He was no scholar, but his father sent him to the monks, who beat enough Latin into him that he could hold his own as an ambassador to His Holiness. But even then, the plan had been for him to sink into the same pit as his father, surrounded by urine and blood and dung and stale beer.

'But you left,' she said, interrupting his memories.

'I ran away.' Finally, witless fool that he was.

'You? What was your plan?'

'I had none. I just…ran.' The last impulsive thing he had ever done. By rights, he should have ended up dead in the gutter of the London streets. Instead, he was picked up from the side of the road by a knight as hungry for adventure as he was. One who appreciated the young boy's ability to wield his brain as well as his sword.

Yet that impetuous act had given him the life he wanted.

'And now you've been all the way to Avignon.' Her voice was as wistful as he had felt as a child when he would escape to watch the road, wishing he could see where it lead.

'Avignon, Calais, Amiens, Toulouse, Bordeaux…' And more. Places whose names he couldn't even remember.

'I envy you.' Her voice, in the dark, brought him back from memories. 'I've never been beyond Lady Joan's household. Not until Canterbury.'

Never been away from her lady. Never seen anything her lady did not also want to see. 'And you wanted to. As much as I did.' His head was beginning to clear.

'You could not understand how much it meant to me to be…free. Just for those few days.'

Ah, but he did. For it was what he had sought all his life. What was finally near his grasp. 'And don't you want more?'

'More? I have food, clothing, shelter. And if I am lucky, a place in heaven. What more could I want?'

'Marriage?' An abrupt question. 'Isn't that something you might want?' He had asked her the question weeks ago. Now, he was not sure what answer he wanted to hear.

She looked down and then back at him, with a smile that said she thought he was a wiser man than that. 'Is it something I might want? As a rabbit might look up at the moon and want to jump there?'

'But…' After a life of being a smooth-tongued diplomat, he found himself speechless. He did not know much of her family, but she was a knight's daughter.

Even if she had little dowry, there might be someone. But she was implying her limp alone would…

Well, it would. Who would want to marry a woman
who could not tramp up and down the castle stairs
or chase the children? Yes, there might be an elusive
'more' to be yearned for, but one must be grateful for
life alone or be willing to face the alternative.

She was right. Food, clothing, shelter…but even
the son of a lowly Lincolnshire tanner had wanted
more than that.

'Even the King wants us to aspire to more. To
chivalry.'

'And to chivalric love? Thus should a lady aspire
to inspire,' she said. 'My lady has certainly done so.'

Her lady. Her lady. 'I have heard all I need to about
Lady Joan. If I have paid my penance, I think I will
find my bed.'

Without hesitation, she thrust her stick into his
hand, as if he, too, might need help to rise.

He did.

And after, he gave her his arm, helped her up and
let her point him in the right direction.

'Why were you here?' he asked, fog finally clear-
ing from his brain. 'Wandering the halls in the dead
of night?'

She leaned on his arm and whispered in his ear,
'The Prince and my lady wanted…time alone.'

And so poor Anne was left to wander the halls.
The anger she refused to feel rose in him. 'But that's
not right.'

'You won't tell the Archbishop, will you?'

Simon Islip had never crossed his mind. All he could think of was Anne and how damned brave and stubborn and selfless she was.

He shook his head. 'Can you return to bed now?'

'I think so. It is near dawn.' She turned and called out behind her, 'Sleep well.'

Behind him, the uneven thump of foot and crutch faded. Then he went down the innumerable stairs, each one a rebuff, and out into the cool air of a September night, and off to find a bed alongside the poor knights in the lower ward.

But he did not sleep. He was thinking of Anne.

Day after day, a woman beyond the blush of maidenhood moved uncomplaining through constant pain. Pain that had etched small lines around lips pursed against it and at the edge of eyes that had winced too often.

Why would he chatter to such a woman about marriage?

It must be the occasion. For weeks, he had been immersed in details of matrimony. What made a marriage official under the church? When was a couple married and when could that be put aside? When would Edward and Joan be allowed to marry? He had been thinking of nothing but marriage. If he had met Anne during the campaign in France, he would have asked her about ships and horse fodder and the price of salted herring.

He rolled on to his back and watched the sky grow light, struggling to control the direction of his foggy thoughts.

He was not a man who would ever marry. Least of all a woman like Anne of Stamford. Yet all the reasons he listed, her infirmity, the burden she would be, not only seemed cruel, they had proven untrue or unimportant.

No, the truth that came to him was more stark.

The truth was, he had nothing to offer her, or any woman, but a strong right arm and a nimble brain. All he had to show for thirty-one years on this earth was the horse beneath him and the armour on his back.

And when he died, there would be nothing to show at all.

Chapter Fourteen

When the King and Queen returned to Windsor for Michaelmas, Edward insisted that the entire court join his inspection of the progress on the new buildings.

Summer was past, the season looked toward winter. But despite the drizzle and the awkward footing in the Upper Ward, Anne enjoyed getting outside, away from detailed discussions of the size of the ostrich feathers and leopards' heads to adorn the red-velvet marital bed.

The mood was festive. Henry the fiddler joined the throng, entertaining those less interested in hearing the clerk of the works discuss the precise angle of the kitchen roof.

The workmen, interrupted, stepped aside to let the King extol his plans. Anne, with a nod of permission from a stonecutter covered with white dust, perched on the block of shaved stone to admire their work.

The new hall and chapel, paid for with French ransoms, were rising against the north wall of the

Upper Ward, grand as a cathedral, and flanked by two gatehouses. Sleeping chambers would be luxurious compared to the cramped quarters within the Round Tower. It would be done soon. And years from now, when Lady Joan became Queen Joan, this would be her home.

And Anne's.

Paid for many times over. Yes, she would be safe here, protected by royal walls, and in a castle where even the passage to the kitchen was protected by a stone tower.

She felt Nicholas beside her before she saw him, and when she looked up, he glanced down at the ground before he met her eyes. He smiled, as tentative as a young page, as if uncertain what to say.

She returned it, equally uncertain.

'How go the plans?' he asked.

'As you might expect,' she said, aware they were surrounded by ears. 'There is much to do. They want all in readiness so they can be wed just as soon as the Pope's dispensation arrives.'

'The Prince asks me twelve times a day when it will come. As if I were the cause of the delay.' He sighed. 'But in all the rush, you hold no needle today.'

She looked down at her fingers, amazed to see them empty. 'I have finished my part. It is the court tailor who is working without rest now.'

Silent, they both looked toward the hall. Robert the Fool ran around the Upper Ward, tripped over a block of stone, or pretended to, then fell flat on his back at Lady Joan's feet. When she leaned over to help and the children clustered around, he bounced to his feet, clapping, and they giggled with glee.

'Does Lady Joan like her new home?' Nicholas asked, finally.

'It has not been much on her mind. First, the wedding. And then…'

'Then, Aquitaine.'

'Where the bridges must be rebuilt.'

His brows rose with surprise.

'Yes, I remember.' Her smile felt soft, at ease, finally, with who they both were.

Quiet for a moment, they listened to the clerk of the works discuss the increased number of fireplaces for the kitchen. Nicholas pulled out one of his cloth balls and tossed it idly for a few moments, then, without warning, threw it to her.

Startled, she fumbled the catch, laughing as it rolled off her skirt and onto the damp grass. She leaned over, scooped it up and threw it back at him, smiling with satisfaction when he dropped the ball.

'The boys,' Nicholas said, a few minutes later. 'Will they go, too?'

She followed his gaze. Lady Joan was surrounded by her four children and the Prince seemed to be lecturing the two boys on the finer points of stag hunting.

'Of course. Where else would they go but with their mother?'

He did not answer and suddenly, she wondered about her assumption. How old were Thomas and

John? Eight? Ten? Old enough to be sent to another household for fostering.

'There will be another son, some day,' Nicholas said, still looking at the boys.

'God willing.' There was no assurance there would be a child, let alone a King, but at least neither was barren. Of that, they had proof.

'They will be with their mother, at least.'

And she knew that Nicholas was thinking of Lady Joan's sons. What would happen when there was another child? How would they fare, being of the King's household, yet not royal?

Would they suffer as Nicholas had?

She reached to touch his sleeve. 'The boys will be cared for.' First, the Prince had been their godfather. Now, he would be their stepfather. He would take the responsibility seriously. 'I am certain of it.'

But what of the girls? Little Joan was nearly the age her mother had been when she wed Thomas Holland, while Maud was not old enough to be let away from the nurse's hand. What would happen to them?

Her lady, Anne had discovered over the years, was drawn to the company of men, no matter what their age. Her daughters were never neglected, her lady was too good for that, but they did not seem to be cherished, as the boys were.

Perhaps it was because she had lost one of her boys.

The King moved on and Anne rose to follow. Nicholas fell into step beside her, kicking chunks of stone and leftover pieces of wood out of her way.

Do not grow comfortable with this, she reminded herself. The Pope's message will come soon. A wedding will be celebrated.

And Nicholas will be gone.

Relieved, Nicholas had seen the Archbishop of Canterbury arrive at Windsor just a few days later, carrying the Pope's message. He had called the Prince and Lady Joan together, closed the door and, Nicholas was certain, extracted the formal and official promises demanded in exchange for permission to wed.

For the next few nights, candles had lit the night as the royal tailor stitched, while minstrels and the chapel singers clashed as they practised.

On the fourth day, Lady Joan declared they were ready. And so, Nicholas found himself in St George's Chapel in Windsor on a bright, October day, as Edward and Joan stood again before the altar. A royal wedding. The only one he was ever likely to see. He had learned from Anne. He would use his eyes to see, to make a memory.

He was not a man to notice the pomp of royal costume, but the golden sparkle of the bride's gown made him blink. Edward and Joan were beaming at each other, with smiles that belonged in the bedchamber, not in the chapel. Standing before them, Archbishop Islip looked slightly sour, but his voice was clear. He was flanked by at least four other churchmen, as if everyone wanted a portion of the honour of marrying England's next King.

The rest of the royal family was there, of course.

If he were any judge, King Edward and Queen Philippa were trying to look pleased. And failing.

Dashed hopes, perhaps on King Edward's part. Mourning lost chances for alliances with more than one Continental kingdom. Or, perhaps, mourning his failure to achieve them. Hadn't those chances been lost long ago? He had not been able to successfully conclude a marriage agreement for his eldest son. What options, really, had been left?

And the Queen—well, he knew little of women, it was true. But her lips seemed tight together, as if it were the only way to keep the semblance of a smile on her face. Joan had been part of her household, raised beside her own children, including Prince Edward. And instead of becoming the model wife and mother that the Queen was, she had disrupted the fabric of church and family not once, but twice, and entangled her son in the second.

Then there was Isabella, Edward's oldest and favourite daughter. The next to be wed, surely. She was nearly of an age with Joan, who had been so reviled for her ancient age. But Joan, at least, had been married. Isabella, at nearly thirty, was still unwed and her father had never seemed eager to find a husband for her.

She had been called wilful, Nicholas had heard.

There were others, aunts, knights and even Joan's children, discreetly off to the side, but despite all the glittering members of the royal family, he found himself looking for Anne.

Anne, the only one who had seen these two married before.

He found her, finally, next to one of Isabella's ladies-in-waiting. Cecily, he thought. The one she said she could laugh with.

Anne managed to stand through the ceremony, as was the custom. He searched her brow and lips for the pinch of pain, but her expression was unusually placid. If she had pain, physical or emotional, she was hiding it well.

He wondered whether she hid other things, as well.

Anne watched the happy couple saying the vows again and felt as if she lived in a dream. The echo of a chapel at midnight. *I, Edward, take thee, Joan...*

And even after all that had happened, after all of Nicholas's assurances, she thought, somehow, that it would not succeed. That God, or the Pope, would refuse permission. After all, there were such good reasons why they should not wed. Reasons which had nothing to do with Joan's other marriages or what Anne knew. The Prince was godfather to her children, now standing below the rail, watching. They shared a grandfather, so were too close to marry. Any of those things should have been enough.

A more inept ambassador, one less skilled than Nicholas, would have failed to convince the Pope to grant an exemption. Or would have failed to persuade the Archbishop to do as the King willed.

Any of those things could have happened and the burden of guilt would have been lifted from her.

Instead, here they were, making a mockery of the laws of God.

And she hadn't stopped it.

And none of them would ever know that the vows now spoken meant that once again, according to the laws of the church, Joan was joined to two men at the same time.

And Anne of Stamford was the only one who knew it.

Chapter Fifteen

The wedding feast lasted the rest of the day, but Nicholas did not feel like celebrating. He was thinking, with regret, it seemed, for the first time, that he would walk away from this wedding alone.

With nothing but the memory of a kiss.

From across the hall, he watched Anne, wondering.

Was she thinking she would never have a husband? She looked over at him and even in the uncertain firelight, he was hit by the yearning in her eyes. For *him*.

A look that drew him back to her side. 'Anne...'

She looked up at him, wary.

'Come. Show me how to look up at the stars and remember tonight.'

She smiled and rose and hobbled beside him, out of the hall and into the ward, close enough to the hall that they could see by the faint light from the windows and hear the muted music of the minstrels. Surrounded by half-timbered buildings backed against the stone walls of the Round Tower, they had only a glimpse of the waxing moon hovering overhead.

Nicholas opened his mouth, uncertain what he wanted to say. 'I'll be leaving soon.' Soon. He could be no more specific.

'Has the ransom come, then?'

He shook his head. 'No, but I don't need to wait.' The Prince's reward would be enough to get him across the Channel and his accounts would wait settlement until the French paid up. Yet he who was so eager to escape had put off doing the things needed so he could.

'Crossing the Channel in winter?' Even Anne knew that was dangerous.

'There is nothing to keep me here.'

'Of course not. You must be eager to leave.'

Was she thinking more? Things she did not say? Against his will, he worried about her, foolishly wanting to be certain she would be safe after he was gone. 'What will happen to you?'

She tilted her head, puzzled. 'Things will go on as they have.' Was there doubt in her eyes? She banished it with a lifted chin. 'Why should it be otherwise?'

She was now the lady of the woman who would be Queen. What safer life could any woman have? And yet... 'If ever something happens. If ever you have a need...'

The laugh. The laugh he had learned was not so merry, but only part of her armour. 'And if I do? Then what? Shall I send a falcon to fly across the Channel and find you on the field in France or Italy or the Golden Horde? Or perhaps pay a messenger to travel for six months in search of you? I doubt my need will be the same a year later, even should he find you and bring you home.'

Home. Home, a place that sounded sharply desirable. He had run from the one he had and never found another, certainly not in England. How much time had he spent on the soil of his birth since he had been knighted on the field in France? Six months? Twelve, perhaps, in ten years.

Yet leaving her alone felt, illogically, wrong. As if he had failed an unspoken obligation. An encumbrance he did not want, and yet…

It was not love. Certainly not. Yet something held him back, heavy as a dead weight on his back. The lure of a woman. Exactly the pull he had so successfully evaded all his life, reaching to trap him.

And he didn't know how to deal with that.

If ever you have a need…

Anne could still hear the echo of his words. Empty words. Yet no one had ever said them to her before. No one except her lady had ever offered a hand of help.

She knew why. Though she asked for nothing, her needs, the needs of a cripple, were too demanding for most people. The chance was great that she would need something a man did not want to give.

And this man? What did he offer but words? Nothing solid. Nothing that would stay.

And yet his kiss.…

She wanted it again, wanted that and more with a hunger stronger than that of her body. Not because no one had ever taken care of her, but because she had been fed and brushed like a horse, without feeling.

Without passion.

And when he said *if you ever need,* she heard passion in his voice. Probably more than he knew, more than he wanted to feel.

No, she could not, would not, ask him to stay. But, oh, just to hear that passion once in her life. To hear the timbre of his voice when he spoke of her. She could do it, just once. She could grab that moment that would not come again and then let him leave, so she would not have to see the regret in his eyes.

Tonight, her lady and the Prince would share their marriage bed. And she would sleep alone. Again and for ever, unless…

Unless…

What harm could there be? Once. Just once before she was returned to her life, never to see anything beyond the reach of her lady's eyes.

She looked at Nicholas again, with all that hunger in her eyes. The kind of hunger she had thought never to fill—for freedom, for distant places, for love. But now, she saw the same from him.

At least, she thought she did, before the cloud trailed across the moon again.

'There is something you can do. Now.'

Surprise in his eyes. How would he look when she told him?

'You said if there was anything I want. There is

something else I want to store in memory.' Her fingers stroked his cheek, softly. 'You.'

Nicholas did not waste breath to ask why she wanted it, nor thought to wonder why *he* wanted it, nor what would come next nor how he would walk away afterwards. He only knew he could not leave without…more. Without taking something of her with him.

So he kissed her.

He was close enough now to catch the scent of her skin. Like pepper and flowers and citron, like Anne herself, tart and sharp on the surface, with the sweetness only revealing itself later.

His lips left hers and trailed down to her throat, bared to him now, her skin smooth and warm. Her breath was short, separated from his lips only by flesh and blood. Her breasts rose and fell, pressing against his chest. For a moment, this was all. This was everything he needed. Wrapped against Anne. Nothing beyond the two of them. No time, no place, beyond this.

Dimly, he felt something surge, stirring in his loins. No, not enough. Not all he needed. He needed so much more of her…

And vaguely, as his body waxed and his mind waned, he understood, as he had not before, about Edward and Joan.

With Nicholas's arms around her, his lips pressed to hers, Anne felt *whole*. As any woman might, able to give and be taken, not out of pity, but from un-holy desire.

She pressed her lips to his, intending to wipe out thought, memory and consequences. She wanted only to savour sensation. The heat of his breath on her cheek. Soft lips. Rough fingers. Her fingers, roaming through his hair, to caress the curve where his neck met his shoulder.

A kiss, she thought. Perhaps more. What could be the harm?

And then, she did not think at all.

Nothing but now. But this. This she must relish. This taste, this feel, tucked away for the long days that would come after.

When she would be alone again.

She had studied stone and glass and stitches, but when she tried to summon logic, to analyse, to name, to commit his scent to memory, to learn the feel of his muscles, beneath wool and skin, she could not control her mind.

She, he, here, now. The taste of foreign lands was on his tongue, the scent so deep in his skin that to be in his arms was a journey, to be held by him was like taking wing. As if all the distant lands she had ever wanted to see were in his arms, soaring as the cathedrals did, arches like hands joined in prayer, reaching to heaven.

His lips left hers and pressed against her vulner-able throat and she gasped for a breath. One more breath. Just one more and one more and one more and then she must let go. She must not reach for things she could never have. God would give her only this one moment, to be paid for later.

As she had been paying for so much all her life.

Did he step away? Did she stumble? Suddenly, they were two people again, separated by inches that might as well have been the miles that would stretch between them as soon as he left. Miles that might as well have been the distance between this world and the next.

Look at him. You must be brave and look at him now.

He tried to speak. 'You asked—'

She touched her fingers to his lips, wanting no words. No regrets.

But instead of silence, he grabbed her hand and pressed his lips against her palm. That simple, tender gesture hurt more than all the thoughts of separation to come.

'Don't.' A single word she could barely utter.

He paused, but did not release her hand. 'I want you.'

She nearly did fall then, not because of her weak leg, but because the force of his desire stole her strength. Had anyone ever desired her before? Ever looked at her with fire in his eyes, with longing?

And that was enough. That would be enough to keep her all the rest of her days. To be with a man who desired her. Once for the rest of her life.

She swayed toward him.

'Lady Anne?' The voice of one of the pages. 'Lady Joan needs you.'

* * *

Nicholas gritted his teeth, trying to force himself back to sense, not stopping to wonder what would have happened if they had not been interrupted. He only knew that he had not wanted to let her go. Not wanted to let the world intrude until he had learned her body as well as the countryside he'd fought over.

Knew that he had nearly been as stupid as his father.

Had it been his loins or his heart talking? Hard to tell one from the other when he looked at her. Which made it so much worse.

Anne made her way back into the hall, suddenly surrounded again by the post-ceremony celebration. The noise and heat of a crowded room. Dancers uneven on their feet, threatening to bump her shoulder or her crutch. Hugs, toasts. Some more genuine than others.

Lady Cecily lifted a goblet to Anne, who paused for breath. She still had half the Hall to cover to reach Lady Joan—no, she must now be called the Princess of Wales—sitting on the dais with the Prince.

'The Princess looks wonderful,' Cecily whispered to her.

'Which one?' Anne said, trying to smile.

'Both of them.' Cecily nodded toward Princess Isabella, who was seated as far away from her brother's new wife as the table would allow.

'Perhaps your lady will be next to wed.' The Princess had reached nearly thirty without a husband. Near as scandalous as her brother.

'My lady will wed if she pleases.' Cecily's voice had an edge. 'A privilege neither of us will see.'

A strange comment, but certainly true. Few men and fewer women married for pleasure. Yet Lady Cecily was fair and whole and from a good family. Strange that she had not yet wed.

Who knew what pain could be disguised behind a healthy body?

The page tugged at her sleeve and she resumed her progress through the Hall. No doubt Edward and Joan were ready to share a bed again, now that they could do so with the church's blessing.

She made her way across the dais and her lady turned away from the table to speak to her. 'I'll be leaving now.'

It was as she had expected, yet her disappointment was sharp. 'I am ready to attend you, of course.' Hair to be combed. Furs to be brushed. Gowns to be put away. The maids must be directed carefully this night.

And Nicholas would be left waiting.

'No.' Joan patted Anne's arm. 'Stay and enjoy yourself. Someone else will attend to me. You have worked very hard, Anne.'

'Thank you, my lady.' Praise that would once have set her smiling. Now, she barely noted the words.

'From now on, the demands there will be, to attend the wife of the future King—well, I do understand they will be beyond what you have been doing.'

She had not complained before. She would not do so now. 'I understand, my lady. I am prepared.' The royal quarters, rising safe and strong, would be the home she had always hoped to have.

'But since St Thomas did not see fit to…' A pause.

'Yes, my lady?' Odd, to hear her lady stumble as she spoke. Perhaps she was tired from the nights of preparations.

'Because of that, I've made arrangements for you to go away for a rest.'

Away. She knew what the word meant, yet it made no sense. Nicholas's kiss must have muddied her hearing. 'Away from you?'

'You need not worry. I will bear all the costs. But doesn't a long rest sound wonderful? I know it has been exhausting, taking care of me all these years. So I've arranged for you to withdraw to Holystone's nunnery.'

'Nunnery?' She had never expected marriage, but to be locked in a convent? No. That she had never, never wanted.

'It is a small one, but I'll arrange a sizeable gift to be sure you are well cared for. And now that the war with Scotland is over, I'm sure it is quite safe, even though it is on the Borders.'

Her lady's meaning was now cold and clear and sharp. The secret Anne had kept for all these years was no longer a protection for her. She was the only one besides Joan who knew the truth. Now that the marriage was finalised, she needed Anne to be far, far away.

Out of sight.
Out of reach.
Locked away like a madwoman.
Silent.

Chapter Sixteen

Speechless, Anne took a step away from her lady, lost in a suddenly spinning world.

How was she to live, torn away from the life that had protected her since childhood?

The answer was simple and brutal. She wasn't.

Oh, it was not an outright threat. Lady Joan would never dream of harming her, of course. It was just that Anne was no longer useful. Worse, she had become… inconvenient. She was the only person to know that the wife of the future King of England, and, more importantly, the mother of a future King of England was not, could not be married to the Prince under church law.

Because she was married to another man.

Only Anne the cripple knew now. And no one would heed her, once she was tucked far away in a convent, never to see the outside world again.

She left the dais and leaned against the wall, unable to take a sure step. The gaiety of the wedding dancers filled the Hall. She had never expected to be able to dance, but to be locked away, never to even see someone else move to music, to hear only music meant for God's ears…

It was not death, exactly. She would still breathe and wake to see the light each day, beckoning outside the convent walls. But she would be trapped, imprisoned in one place more tightly than her leg could ever have held her.

As tight as a coffin might hold her.

'You do not seem happy.' Nicholas had appeared beside her, without her even knowing. 'What did she want?'

She must keep smiling. 'Just to thank me. Of course I am happy. For her.'

'And for yourself?'

She looked away. 'I have nothing to complain of.' And yet she wanted to complain, to keen in mourning at the loss of her world. A world in which once, at least, a man had kissed her. 'But I have some things I must tell you.'

Within days, he would be gone from her life for ever. The only man who had ever really seen her. She had thought to make a memory tonight, but perhaps she would repay a debt instead.

Staying close to the wall, Nicholas guided Anne out of the Hall. Revellers were spilling out of the Hall, looking for fresh air, and the yard that had been theirs before was now dotted with other couples.

He found quiet shelter in the stairway, where

torches studded the walls so that guests would not miss a step and tumble down the stairs cascading below them.

They settled on one of the steps and Nicholas brushed the hair away from Anne's brow, wanting to take her lips again, but her mood had shifted. The moment lost.

She took a breath. 'Tonight is goodbye.' Her voice was steady. Steadier than he felt. Now he was the one whose legs seemed too weak to carry him forward. He did not want to examine why.

'I do not leave yet.'

'I do.'

Shock. Where would she be going? 'I thought the Prince and Princess would remain at Windsor.'

'They will. I go alone.'

'Alone?' An echo, that word. She had never gone anywhere alone. 'Where?'

She pursed her lips, looking not at him, but down the stairs that disappeared into darkness. 'To the convent of Holystone.'

He'd never even heard the name. 'Where is that?'

She shrugged. 'Northumberland. Near the Borders.'

None of the words made sense. 'On a mission for your lady?'

A deep breath, then Anne met his eyes again. 'My lady thinks I need a rest.'

'Do you?' The words were sharper than he had intended.

She shrugged.

Something was wrong. Why was she going alone

to a desolate, dangerous wasteland? She had wanted to travel, especially without her lady, but there was no excitement in her voice. 'Is it what you want?'

'It is…better that I go.' She looked down the stairs that would take her away. In the flickering torchlight, they almost seemed to move. 'I have been with Lady Joan a long time. I remind her of too many things.'

He sensed treacherous ground here. 'What things?' He asked as if it were his right to know.

She did look at him then, long and hard and silent, as if she were making a hard decision. 'Of the past. You asked me once if I knew who witnessed her marriage to Holland. I do. It was my mother. My mother was the witness.'

If he had been standing, he would have fallen.

He tried to reorder the pieces, to fit together everything he had learned, confirmed and did not know.

A clandestine marriage with a witness. And all his questions had come to naught. It had seemed strange at the time, but she had insisted she did not know.

He grabbed her shoulders and shook her. 'I asked you and you lied.' Anger doubled, for lie upon lie. He should not have been surprised. And yet… 'Why didn't you tell me?'

She looked down at her lap. 'I have never told anyone.' Her words were a whisper, as if she did not want to tell him either.

Yet here, breathing the scent of her, knowing this would be the last time he would see her, his anger shattered.

He let his hands slip off her shoulders and gathered her fingers in his. 'Tell me.'

With her fingers tight in his, Anne felt at once safe and trapped. She had led him this far, exchanged a night of passion for a night of truth, or partial truth, uncertain whether she was looking for redemption, forgiveness, or simply a witness.

The top of Nicholas's head met hers as they looked down at their clasped fingers. 'Where were they? When they married?' he whispered, the words muddied as they bounced against the walls and down the stairs.

This part was easy to tell. She had repeated it many times. 'Flanders.'

'Why were they in Flanders?'

'Thomas Holland went in the retinue of the Earl of Salisbury. He was part of the embassy of earls and bishops sent to present the King's statement of grievances to Philip of France.'

Nicholas nodded. 'And Joan?'

His question was sharp. He might not forgive her for this, but then, it would not matter now.

'The following summer. She was not yet ten and still in the care of the Queen, so when she came to Flanders to join the King, Joan and some of her children came, too.'

'And your mother? Why was she there?'

'Serving the Queen.' She could see him about to ask the next question. 'She brought me with her.'

'You couldn't have been…'

'Barely born. She could have left me with a wet nurse, but the Queen brought some of her own children, as well as Joan, too, so she could not force Mother to leave me behind. Already, they could tell I was not going to be…' still hard to say '…like other children.' A smile now. 'We were there for three years, travelling with court.'

'In the midst of a war.' His sigh said he knew exactly what that meant. 'At least I was never asked to find food and lodging for the Queen as well as for fighting men.'

She nodded. 'It was difficult. An Abbey one night. A peasant's house another. Some nights, we did not know where we would be sleeping. Mother was supposed to watch over Joan, but it was hard. Some nights…'

Some nights, no one was certain where Joan slept.

She could see understanding dawn on his face. 'And Holland was there?'

'By late summer of the third year, I think. Mother told me, but it is hard to remember clearly.'

'You were a babe.'

'Nearly four by then. But it was clear…' She looked down at her leg. 'Mother had her hands full with me. The Queen had three of her own children with her. No one had much extra time to mind the Lady Joan.'

'If she was twelve, she was a maiden of age, capable of taking care of herself,' he said, with a cynical edge to the words. 'But Holland was a fully fledged fighting man by then.'

She nodded. 'Six and twenty. And weary of the

battle, I'm sure. They had a victory at sea, then a defeat on land. The King and his men were in Ghent, frustrated, short on funds and trapped. The King had to escape in the dark, leaving the Queen and the rest of us behind as hostages. No one knew when we might see home again.'

She remembered none of it well. None of it except the fear.

'And that was when…?'

She nodded.

'Men at war lack…control.' The grim set of his lips told her he understood. 'Did he even woo her?'

'I don't know. But he was dashing and had served as the King's lieutenant in Brittany. No doubt he would have drawn a young maiden's eye.' But then, most men drew Lady Joan's attention. Anne imagined it had always been so.

'And she his?'

She gripped her hands together. It was hard to talk of this part, particularly after she and Nicholas had just…

'Mother told me that one night, she stumbled into a dark corner of the Abbey where they were staying and saw the two of them together and they were…'

There was no question, her mother had told her later. No other explanation for what they were doing. He was fully plunged between her spread legs, her skin white in contrast to the dark wool hose he hadn't bothered to remove. Joan looked up, horror on her face, trying to scramble away, begging forgiveness immediately.

Thomas, being a man, took longer to come to his senses.

She tried to explain. 'But they had not, Thomas had not fully...' She knew not how to describe something she had never experienced.

Nicholas coughed and cleared his throat. 'And then what?'

She had wondered that, exactly, for years. But the Joan she knew always tried to please. First, perhaps, to please Anne's mother. Then, to please Thomas Holland. 'She apologised. She promised it would never happen again. But Mother said that Holland grabbed the girl's hand, swore an oath that they were married and she matched it with her vow. "Wait for me," he said. He said he would come for her. That they would be together.'

Nicholas scoffed. 'A man still in heat who had not released his seed? He would have promised anything.'

She blushed. 'My mother thought the same.'

'And she told no one?'

'Joan begged her not to, so Mother held her tongue. What else could she do? If she told the truth, it would only mean ruin for all.' She lifted her eyes to his. 'So, when Holland returned and Mother was asked, later, whether they had married, Joan gave her permission to tell.'

'Why didn't you tell me before?' He looked... hurt. As if she had owed him the truth. 'When you knew...?'

'Knew what? I knew what my mother told me. I

was not the witness. Yet I knew they were married. And that everything was as it had been said.'

'Would you have told me if it weren't?'

She should never have said even this much. She had raised suspicions safely laid to rest, but with him, it had always been hard to lie.

But she would. Even now, she would. All would be as it must. 'Do you doubt it? You did what was asked. You are free to leave. To return to France, a man content.'

Yet he did not look content. 'And suddenly, after a lifetime, Joan wants to forget all this by putting you out of sight?'

'You must understand. Lady Joan will be the Queen. No Queen has ever had such a history. It is still a…difficult matter.'

'Difficult!' He raised his brows and his voice. 'I travelled to Avignon and Canterbury and back for this marriage. Don't tell me how difficult it is.'

She must throw him off. 'What I mean is that some people… Memories are long…' Did she look close to tears? Would he reach over and touch her, forgiving?

She had learned too much from the Lady Joan.

'You do not want to go.' It was not a question.

Too perceptive, Nicholas Lovayne. She looked away, too late, for he had already seen the truth. 'No. I do not.'

And she would soak up as many memories as she could before they locked her behind the walls.

At the top of the stairs came a woman's laughter, with a man's. The sound of a kiss.

Nicholas coughed and the laughter disappeared, back into the courtyard and the night.

'You don't have to go,' he said then. 'You could…'

'I could what?' She glanced down at her leg, invisible beneath her skirt. Here was the choice her mother had faced. What could such a child do? What would become of her when her family was gone and there was no one to care for her? Her mother had made the choice she thought would protect Anne and, until now, it had.

She turned, lifting her face to his. 'You must promise me something. You must do it for me. When you leave, when you go back to France and Italy and the rest of the world, look at it twice as hard. Look at it for yourself and then look at it for me. Look at every leaf and stone and bit of coloured glass and every wave. And know that I will think of you. That I am here, imagining all the wonders the world holds.'

And praying that God would forgive her ingratitude for the mercy he had shown her. Her ingratitude in wanting things she was never meant to have.

He reached for her hand. 'Send a page when you are ready,' he said. 'I shall take the journey with you. I will see you safely there.'

Chapter Seventeen

Anne pulled away. 'No. You are kind, but I do not want to hold you back.' She waved a hand. 'France, Italy, Spain await you.'

'And a small, stone building on the windswept edge of the kingdom awaits you. Let me take you there. And on the way, we will see something…something you want to see before…'

Before she would see nothing more.

But Nicholas was not so blunt as to say it. 'What would it be?' His question was eager. 'Where can I take you?'

She wanted to say nowhere. She wanted to say everywhere. She wanted to say the story had been a parting gift, even though she had lied to him.

She had lied all her life, the weight of it as heavy as the dead weight of the foot she dragged behind her. And even if she were foolish enough to tell the truth and he were foolish enough to forgive her, it would not lift the weight of all those years of lies.

And the more he did for her, the kinder he became, the heavier the weight of her lie.

She shook her head. 'You have delayed already. I know you want to go.'

'No one is waiting for me. A few weeks won't matter.'

A few weeks. She had thought only tonight, but to have a few weeks… And so she succumbed to temptation. A few more weeks. A few more memories of Nicholas.

'Pick something,' he said, when she remained silent.

She closed her eyes, imagining the whole kingdom and not knowing which piece to pick. What even lay between here and Holystone? The joy would be the discovery.

'A cathedral,' she said, finally.

'But you just saw a cathedral. In Canterbury.'

She smiled. Nicholas had not yet learned how to look at a cathedral. 'Each one is different. Each is a miracle. Stone soaring to heaven. Coloured glass more beautiful than imaginings. Jewels. All created by man as a gift from the earth back to the God who created it.'

He studied her and for a moment, she feared he could see it all. 'A cathedral, then. Any particular one?'

Oh, if she had the world and time, she would stop at each one. 'Any one we find.'

A few weeks more and then…

She would not think beyond that.

Nor of how she would say goodbye.

* * *

Thinking about it the next morning, Nicholas didn't know why he had insisted that he take Anne to Holystone. He had finished his work. She had even given him the answer to the final, troubling mystery of the witness to Lady Joan's first marriage to Holland. All was answered. All was in order.

And if there had been kisses, they had been given freely. She had given him leave to go.

Yet, he didn't. Something held him back in a way he did not recognise and did not particularly like.

Most of his life had been lived with his mind fully in control, guided by a clear purpose. Now, he found himself on a battlefield where body, heart and mind waged perpetual war.

She had crept beneath his armour and he was perilously close to acting the fool for a woman, just as his father and the Prince had. He had already been foolish enough to delay his departure for weeks, all because he didn't trust anyone else to properly care for her on her journey.

His leavetaking of the Prince was brief and included Lady Joan. The two emerged from their chamber, finally, beaming, with barely a thought or a glance to spare for anyone besides each other.

'You'll be back to us before Yuletide, then?' the Prince asked, when Nicholas had explained his journey.

Nicholas nodded. 'Well before.' A month to get there and back, perhaps more, though as autumn stretched toward winter, travel would grow treacherous.

'Then you will celebrate with us,' the Prince said, with the smile of a man ready to establish a home. 'At Berkhamsted.'

Joan stepped forward, putting her fingers on Nicholas's sleeve. An intimate little gesture, though it somehow seemed planned.

When had he become so doubtful of a woman everyone else called beautiful and good? At the same time he had allowed himself to become emotional about Anne?

'Thank you,' Joan began, her voice pitched low, 'for offering to take good care of my Anne. I think… after all these years…she is just weary. She needs a rest.'

The words would have made sense, had he not known Anne as he did. She never rested. Her fingers worked, even when her legs did not. And when she did rest, her eyes were busy, drinking in every bit of what surrounded her, so that she could relive it later.

And he wondered whether he had underestimated Lady Joan. Originally, he had thought her slightly empty-headed. Lovely, but without the capacity to understand and manage complexities. Now, he was not certain.

He inclined his head, acknowledging her care. 'I am certain you will miss her, my lady.'

'Of course. We have been close for so many years.'

'So I understand. When will she be coming back?'

'Oh, not until she wants to. I will not pressure her.'

Nothing suspicious in that answer, nor in her smile. Yet there was one way to test the truth of her. The risk was that she would be even more angry at Anne. But if he were right… 'Since Flanders, wasn't it?'

Her eyes became like daggers. 'Flanders?'

'When she was but a babe. You must have cared for her when her mother was busy with the Queen's children. Her mother was close to you, as well, wasn't she?'

The least bit of panic touched her eyes. 'Ah, did Anne tell you that?'

A warning. Enough for him to protect Anne. 'I can't remember. Perhaps it was something the Queen mentioned when I was preparing to visit His Holiness.'

'Well, all that is behind us now, isn't it?' She dusted his sleeve, as if there had been a speck of dirt on it.

As easily as she was dusting Anne out of her life.

Lady Joan turned back to the Prince. 'If Nicholas is taking her north, you will not need to send any of your men, will you?'

The Prince looked to Nicholas, who smiled.

'I'm certain that my squire and her maid will be enough,' he said, fiercely glad that Anne would have someone on this journey who cared about her.

So in the fullness of a cool, sunny, October day, Anne, firmly attached to her gentle jennet, rode north beside Nicholas, followed by Eustace and Agatha.

She tried to inhale the vision so that she could re-member it always. The piercing blue sky. Leaves of wild red and gold and brown. The air, sweet on her cheeks. The horse, warm and solid beneath her. None of this would she know again.

'Are you all right?' he asked. 'To ride?'

She nodded. It was not easy. It would never be easy. But the trip to Canterbury had built her muscles and her skills. And it would be the last time she would see any of this. For that, it was worth any pain.

For that, and to steal these final, precious days with Nicholas.

The King had given them leave to stay at his palaces on their way, so the end of the first day's travel seemed little different than when she journeyed with the court, except that she did not spend her waking hours with an eye out for what the Lady Joan might want.

As a result, she noticed that Nicholas's squire and Agatha seemed to spend an inordinate amount of time within touching distance of each other. And when it was time for bed, Agatha appeared with rumpled hair and short of breath, a look Anne now recognised.

'Agatha,' she began, 'you know that Eustace will be a knight soon.'

The girl nodded. 'Within the year, he hopes. As soon as he and Sir Nicholas join the Great Company and he can prove himself...' Her words faded and she bit her lip, knowing she had revealed too much.

My fault. Anne winced. Keeping not only Nicholas but his squire from their glory. And putting a simple young girl's heart in harm's way. 'And you also know,' she said, 'that a knight will never wed a serving girl.'

'Wed?' She cocked her head. 'I never thought so.'

Now Anne felt as if she were the simple one, thinking that a man's kiss would mean more than momentary pleasure. This girl had learned a lesson Anne had not. 'So you don't expect...'

Agatha did not wait for her to find the word. 'I don't let tomorrow's trouble sour today.'

And hadn't Anne done exactly that? She had taught Nicholas to see, to create something to remember, yet she had let her fears prevent her from relishing the days she had left.

That would change.

So she asked him, the next morning, as the open road stretched before them, what cathedral they would see. She had travelled with the court, but had only a misty notion of place and direction. Only that Holystone would be far, far away.

'Which one?' Nicholas smiled. 'Ely, Lincoln, York, Durham? All of them!'

Laughter rolled through her, like a thunderstorm passing by in spring. 'All of them?'

'Why not?'

'Because we would be travelling until Yuletide.' She would not have minded that. She would not have minded travelling beside him for ever. She let the moment, and the wish, fade. 'You have postponed your life for me long enough. One. We will pick one cathedral.'

He did not argue, but she wasn't certain he agreed. 'Ely is the first one. We will see Ely.'

And she thought there was one more memory she would take from this journey.

* * *

They could not help but see Ely Cathedral, Nicholas thought, as they approached the town a few days later.

The Cathedral shimmered in the distance near half a day before they arrived. The land was flat here and the Cathedral's tower taller than the trees on the horizon, almost like a ship, sailing over the marshy fens.

They had travelled slowly. Nicholas had wanted to be certain they had lodgings each night so Anne would not have to sleep outdoors. She had complained of nothing, protesting that she could sleep anywhere, but there was another reason that he had not shared with her.

It kept her more safely away from him.

Kisses were one thing. But he wanted more than that now. Things he must not have.

There was no castle near Ely, so he arranged for lodgings, making sure that Anne could sleep alone, and left Eustace and Agatha to unload so he and Anne could explore the church while there were no services.

They entered the great doors and paused, looking down the great nave.

'How does this compare to Chartres?' Anne whispered, as if not to disturb God.

He shrugged. 'I don't know.'

'But you saw it. You told me so when we were in Canterbury.'

'I was there. I did not see it,' he said, realising it was the truth. He had stood before it, walked inside it, even waited behind the King as the treaty was hammered out and signed, but he could no more summon up a vision of it than of any of the countless other buildings he had seen in France.

'Show me Ely, Anne. Show me so I will know I was here.'

'Just look,' she said, as if impatient with a balky student. 'How many towers has it?'

'One.'

'Yes. Only one. Most churches have two.'

He nodded. Something else he had *seen* without ever really *seeing*.

'Now look, there.' She pointed at the top of the arches lining the nave. 'You see the carvings up there?'

Not until she had shown them to them.

'They are of the saint, Etheldreda.'

He squinted to see the place where the columns met the arches. Had he ever noticed anything other than how many men could sleep in a castle's hall and whether the list he had given matched the food delivered?

So many things that he had not seen. Excited, she did not wait for him to catch up. 'And the windows, you see? Angels playing music.'

He tried to make out the image. Once he opened his eyes, once he tried to see it all, there was too much to take in.

But already she was pointing out something new. 'Now look up. Have you ever seen anything like that?'

Above him stretched eight arches, meeting to support a higher structure, floating above the floor. It must have been the dome-like structure they had seen before they even reached the city. It looked as celestial and far above the world as if God had made it and put it in the heavens. Standing directly beneath it, he was dizzy.

Yes, he would remember Ely Cathedral now.

What would the rest of the world look like, through Anne's eyes? Something to be savoured, rather than endured. To be lingered over instead of passed over. Every place he planned to visit would be different if she were there, if he were travelling slowly enough to notice...

He was still thinking of that, with a moment's pang for the Canterbury badge he had dropped, at day's end when they had returned to the inn.

Through supper, Anne told Eustace and Agatha of everything they had seen until the young people finally made their escape. Alone with Nicholas, having re-examined it all, she fell silent as he tossed one of his juggling balls from one hand to the other. Finally, by mutual consent, they rose and he carried a candle to light her way as she took the stairs, one at a time.

In front of her door, she paused. 'Etheldreda was from Northumberland, you know,' she said.

He shook his head. 'No. I didn't.'

'I wonder if she missed it.' Anne was whispering now, barely talking to him at all.

He had no answers for her. From what he had heard, Northumberland was a cold, windswept, barren land, best left to the quarrelling Borderers who lived there.

Italy, at least, would be warm.

But Anne was looking at him now, with an intensity that spoke of the rest of her life. 'She also died a virgin.'

He looked around, grateful that they were alone. He cleared his throat. 'Really?'

'She had two husbands and she died a virgin. I won't have even one, but I don't want...' Looking right at him now. 'Would you...?'

Of all the questions she had asked him, this was the easiest one to answer. He had longed to hold her once more since the night of the royal wedding.

Yet without his intention, his gaze drifted to all that was hidden beneath her skirt.

The edge of her mouth ticked upwards. 'It is only my foot. Besides that, I am like other women.'

Embarrassed, he realised she knew what he had been thinking. 'But you haven't, you don't mean—?'

'No! I have not... I am not a woman who has attracted men that way. But once, I would like just once...'

That, he could give her.

They could not run. Here. It must be here. Now. If they waited until it was easy or convenient, he, both of them might come to their senses. And for once, that was not what he wanted.

He opened the door to her room, and held out his hand.

Chapter Eighteen

I must remember everything, Anne thought, as the door closed behind them. *Every moment so that I can relive it later.*

Until Nicholas, she had known nothing of loving or kisses. Yet she had spent a lifetime near a woman who loved men. Lady Joan had borne Thomas five children. Some nights, Anne had heard them, through the door. The panting, the groans, the screams. And with the Prince, it was the same.

But for herself, beyond the kisses she had shared with Nicholas, there was only the mystery of *want.*

He put the candle down beside the bed and she looked at the straw mattress, hesitant to take that step. *Now. It must be now.*

Suddenly, he scooped her into his arms and carried her there and all her awkwardness fell away.

Tonight, she would be the Anne she was inside.

Nicholas sat beside her on the bed and looked at her, head to toe, without speaking. The silence lengthened, her cheeks grew hot and she looked away, unaccustomed to being examined instead of overlooked.

He reached for the fall of her hair and lifted it behind her shoulder to reveal her face.

Her breathing quickened. 'What are you doing?'

A gentle smile in answer. No need to be urgent this night.

'Looking at your hair,' he said. 'It is one of my favourite parts of you.'

Foolish flattery. 'Red hair is frowned on.'

He furrowed his brow and skewed his lips into mock consideration. 'Then I will not call it red. Shall I name it sanguine? Or gules? What shall I call it?'

'Call it nothing at all. Don't look at it at all.'

'You've taught me to see.' His fingers played with her hair, a gesture as intimate as if he was stroking her skin. 'Yet you do not want to be seen?'

No. She did not. She wanted to close her eyes and disappear into him, consumed by this mysterious thing between men and women.

'You have always seen me more clearly than others do.' *Be brave. Look at him.* But she could not.

'That's what I want to do. I want to spend this night looking at you, from head to—'

'No! You must promise me.' She bent her knees, drawing up her legs hiding her foot, still in its red hose, safely beneath her skirt. 'Don't look…'

And of course, he did. 'I've already seen it. You don't have to hide.'

But she did, she had to hide so many things. 'Don't

look at me at all.' She leaned over and, with one breath, the candle went dark.

Outside, the sun had set. Fading light still smudged the room, but she felt safer now. More hidden. Less Anne.

He inhaled, as if to argue, and then her lips took his and there were no more words.

He broke the kiss and pulled off his tunic and hose. In the near dark, she was brave enough to shed all but her chemise, letting him help.

She felt his hands stroke her arms, explore her neck and she could scarcely breathe for the joy of it.

A human touch. She had not realised that skin could crave such a thing. Air, velvet, linen, silk, sun—all had stroked her skin without her notice.

But when had any man ever touched her with tenderness, with passion?

Touched her at all?

Now, everywhere, his fingers, lips, as if kindling flame wherever he touched. She succumbed to the feeling, to being pleasured, and then, as he cupped her hip, stroked her thigh, she tensed.

No lower. He must not go lower…

'Shh. I promise.'

And because she believed him, she let the want crash through her.

Soft surprise, to discover how alive she could feel. Skin, breath, something even deeper trembling, fighting to break free, escape, faster than a horse could gallop, mobile as a falcon in flight. Soaring. Never, never wanting to touch earth again.

Here, now, finally, she was not slow or awkward. She did not stumble or hobble. Nothing held back her kisses or her touches.

Even though she had never loved a man before, it felt easy and natural. As if she were not the Anne everyone saw, but the Anne she had always wanted to be.

Free.

This, Nicholas knew he would remember.

Don't look at me, she had begged. Yet as the last light of dusk ebbed from the room, he filled his eyes with the sight of her face, lips parted, eyes half-closed, freed of pain and worry, feeling only the pleasure of his touch.

He explored her skin with gentle fingers and watched her stretch and sigh and offer herself for more. His lips took the tip of one breast and she moaned in delight. Trailing kisses, he discovered one, then the other, the same, yet different, until he was certain he would know one from the other, even in the dark.

Now came the curve of her hips. A kiss where a bone lay beneath skin impossibly fair and pale. Skin no man had ever seen.

Her belly next, and a kiss for the dip of her navel, the centre of a woman's wantonness. Yet she did not writhe, as he expected. Instead, she laughed, truly and lightly, with only the rounded edges of joy. And at that, he laughed, as well, as glad to coax her joy as her passion.

The passion would come.

Her legs next, for him to explore, but as he went lower, she tensed, so he stopped, and let her pretend that she could move as freely as any other woman.

Here, she could.

Her thighs were firm beneath his palms, the muscles grown strong from days of gripping the horse. But between them, ah, between her thighs he would find the seat of her passion.

A kiss there, too. A kiss on her secret centre. No hesitation now. No resistance. She opened to him, her slick scent showing that she was ready.

But he was not. He wanted to savour this moment, to relish her release instead of his own. He wanted to see her face when she felt for the first time that shift in the earth that signalled she had crossed to the other side.

And so, instead of taking her, he led her. First, with his tongue and kisses, tasting her sweetness, loving the sound of her breathing, shorter, faster. Then, because he wanted to miss nothing, he moved his kisses higher until he could look at her face again.

Her eyes, still closed, fluttered open. Then, a smile.

'Yes,' she whispered. 'Now.'

And he did not take his eyes from hers as he slipped inside her.

Anne had thought she understood something of lovemaking. But as Nicholas filled her, she realised she had known nothing at all.

Man and woman did not fit together as two people who clasped hands, but remained in their own bodies. Instead, they merged into one being, no longer separate. He breathed in. She exhaled. His heart beat. So did hers. He pulsed within her and she answered, over and again, higher and faster and stronger.

And then, the strength exploded into shards of shining weakness and in that, too, she knew they were as one.

Nicholas awoke feeling as if his world was upside down.

Anne still slept beside him, but restless, he left the bed, pacing, realising quickly how small the room was.

Standing as far away as he could, he looked at her, curled atop the bed. Her pale reddish-blonde hair hung over the side of the mattress. Her foot was safely hidden beneath the covers, but the red woollen hose that had covered it had escaped and lay tangled in the linens.

And he thought of last night.

He had prided himself on many things during his life, but this, knowing that his lips, his fingers, had brought her such joy...

This made him feel finally, truly, a man.

He had taken women before, but he had taken them as he had ridden over the land, barely stopping to glance at it on the way. Were they fair or dark? Round or sharp? It did not matter. Each was only there to get him where he wanted to go.

But Anne…

It did not matter that the room was dark. He would know her anywhere now. Her scent. The curve of her hips, one different from the other, as each had a different job to do. He had traced her pale eyebrows now, memorised them with his fingers, learned the shape of her jaw by kissing it, imprinted her body on his own as if he were earth.

No woman had ever given herself to him so freely, without expecting anything in return. He had thought he would have to coax her. To tease her slowly, to lead her bit by bit. A touch on the hand, then on the neck. A soft kiss first. He had thought that passion would have to wait, as he drew her in.

Instead, the barest touch, the first meeting of lips and tongue, and all the hesitation was gone. She had yielded, pressing herself to him as if he were her returning lover, coming home from the war.

When in his life had he ever given himself so completely? When had he ever known a woman so completely?

If he never saw her again, he knew he would carry the memory until the day he died.

If…

There was no 'if'. There was only the certainty that he must take her, as he promised, to a small, cold convent near the end of the world and leave her there, far away from the very world she hungered to experience.

He could not leave her.

Could not or would not?

To the Prince, of course, he had owed his duty.
There was no duty here. There was only…

He refused to think the word. The woman was
nothing to him. She would tie him down, even more
than an ordinary woman.

And he was trapped by the argument, unable to do
anything but watch her and wait for her to wake, not
knowing what would happen when she did.

Anne knew she waked, but she squeezed her eyes
tighter, not wanting to face the dawn. Oh, she had
given herself last night and she had no regrets. It was
better than riding a horse, or chasing a hawk. It was
as if her own, poor body could fly.

Oh, it had been more awkward, she supposed, than
it would have been for some women, as he honoured
his promise and did not look at or touch her foot, but
at the end, it was as if her spirit, at once in her body
and mingling with his in the air, was no longer felt
trapped.

That was the memory she had wanted. That was
the memory she would cherish in the long, dark days
to come.

The bed was empty, but she heard his breath, near
the hearth.

Life. Life must be resumed.

Stretched on her stomach, she pushed herself up
on her elbows and looked at him, her breath catching in her throat all over again. She had felt him all
over, but in the dark tumble beneath the covers she
had not *seen* him.

Not like this.

Now, she could see those legs. As long and straight as she had imagined, and yet the thighs…well, now she knew. The strength it took to sit on a horse.

And the curves she had caressed on his shoulders and arms, smooth like the worn steps of Canterbury, now she could see the blue of his veins, strong as a river, coursing beneath his skin.

She would remember this, exactly. Later.

'Thank you,' she said.

He opened his mouth and shut it, for once without words.

She felt, now, that her foot was naked and she sat up, looking frantically for the sock to cover it. 'Don't look,' she warned, before she pulled her foot from under the covers, and he sighed, but turned his head.

Covered again, she tried to swing her leg around, suddenly awkward, all freedom and grace of last night gone. Immediately, he was there, settling her with a touch, as if he knew just how to help without making her feel clumsy.

Oh, the tenderness in just that simple gesture. Equal to every passionate touch from last night.

He sat beside her and turned her face to his. 'Anne…'

She jerked away from his hands. 'No words. What are words compared to what happened last night? Nothing.' Weak, worthless things.

'But everything has changed.'

'Nothing has changed.' All gone. All the joy of the

memory. Not to be visited again until she was safely away from him. 'Everything will be as it must.'

He rose, pacing again. Ah, how she envied him those simple steps. 'As it must? Or as Lady Joan wills it?'

Anne gripped the bedpost and pulled herself to her feet. 'Or the Prince or the King or the Pope.'

'What about what Anne wants?'

The sad smile came before she could stop it. 'I know what Nicholas wants. Nicholas wants freedom. Nicholas wants to roam the earth of France or Italy or Castile or even Cyprus. Nicholas wants to roam unfettered.' She bit her lip.

And so did she.

'So Nicholas,' she continued, 'will do as he said he would and take me to Holystone to rest. Then, he will be free.'

Oh, the ache that word put in her throat.

She could not read his face clearly, but she saw a struggle there. Some tug of war between what he wanted and what he...desired.

'I am not a man who falls in love.'

'I know.' And now for the lesson Agatha had taught her. 'I am not a woman who expects love.' Wants it, yes. Oh, yes. But she had known, always, there would not even be marriage, let alone passion. 'This was one night. A gift.' A memory to be taken out and relived when the cold walls of her sister cell closed in on her like the short, dark winter days.

And then his eyes warmed. 'Not just one. We will have more nights to come.'

Chapter Nineteen

So they made their way north, not hurrying, pretending to each other that the journey would not end.

And if they went a few miles afield to see a cathedral or enjoy a market day, what was the harm? Anne refused to dwell on it. Refused to think of anything beyond the day. And the night.

And if she had a child? She would not think of that, either. She would be safely locked away, the babe cared for in the convent, and no one beyond those walls would ever know.

With no one to stitch for, her hands were empty, so in the evenings Nicholas taught her to juggle. Or tried to. She learned to toss two balls, and the other guests at the inn applauded the night she finally succeeded with three.

And afterwards they went up the stairs together, letting the others think they were married.

Eustace and Agatha kept their secret.

* * *

'We will be in Lincoln tomorrow,' Nicholas said, late one night a week later, as they lay together, sated and warm.

She snuggled closer. 'Beyond the scent of the tannery, I hope.' She had not seen it, but the stench had hovered in the air most of the day.

Beside her, he went still and quiet. 'Yes. Well beyond.'

She nodded and drifted toward sleep. Then, something he had said, long ago, tickled her memory. 'Is your home near? Would you show me?' He had no family left, she remembered that, so there would be no awkward explanations to make.

She rolled on to her back and tapped his nose with her finger. 'I'd like to picture you there as a little boy.' She giggled. 'Learning to juggle. Show me where you learned to juggle.'

Abruptly, he turned away and sat up on the edge of the bed. 'Why would you want to see that?'

'Because I care about you.' She trailed her fingers down his bare back.

He moved again, standing, out of reach of her hand. 'Because you are trying to trap me.'

'Trap you?' She shook her head, thinking her sleep-fogged brain must be confused. 'How… Why… What…?'

Nicholas was pacing now, as if he wanted to escape the room. 'Yes. Trap me, force me into marriage.'

Something cold, as if she were frozen, trickled under Anne's skin. 'How can you think—?'

'Isn't that what you want? You would be saved from the convent and I'd be weighed down with a wife.'

She could not speak, then, for the pain that gripped her.

Weighed down. Cannot move.

And if she had ever, in the moments before sleep, dreamed of tomorrows with Nicholas, she had known it was impossible. For her, but most of all for him. How could he accuse her when she had tried so hard?

She lashed out, speaking no more sense than he. 'You were the one who insisted that you come with me.' A worse thought now. 'Did you do it only because you could take what you wanted? No one would know or care what happened to me, would they?'

And everything she had cherished seemed about to turn to ash and bitter words.

Nicholas saw Anne's stricken face, suddenly sharp and clear, and it brought him back to himself. What had happened? One moment he had been holding her tight, grateful that more than half the journey still lay before them, wishing he never had to leave her. The next—

The next he was a child again, wanting to escape a home that did not want him, resenting a father who had let a woman deceive him.

Trapped. It was his stepmother he spoke of. He had been running from his father's fate all these years and not realised it until now.

He knelt by the bed and raised a hand to Anne's cheek. 'I'm sorry. I didn't mean—'

She swatted it away. 'Spare me your apologies.'

He grabbed her hands back. 'Please. Let me tell you.'

Silent, she glared at him, trying to hide the hurt behind a defiant stare. Finally, she spoke, slowly, each word with a weight of its own. 'I…don't…care.'

But he would not let her go. He could see what held her back, but something had weighed him down, too. Something she could not see.

He began to speak, as if she had said nothing, keeping her hands in his so she could not cover her ears. 'My father was a tanner.'

There, the surprise on her face. 'And you, a knight?'

How far he had come. Almost far enough to forget the stench of the pits where the skin was separated from the fat and flesh. It had taken him years to run far enough away to clear that smell from his nostrils.

But there was more to tell. 'My mother died when I was a babe. I barely remember her.'

Sympathy softened her face. Her mother must have been her whole world. He envied her that.

Then, the flicker of feeling was gone. 'You told me this before,' she said. 'Or were you too drunk to remember that?'

'I told you, but I did not tell you all.'

There was something he could not read in her expression, but she remained silent and waited for him to continue.

'And then, my father, instead of being sensible and

marrying a woman with a dower, fell in love with a woman near half his age. She led him on—' the words bitter even to this day '—pretending to be a shy and chaste maiden, and he let lust rule him. He pressured her parents to allow them to wed quickly. And five months after they were wed, I had a younger brother.'

And that quickly, his father's dreams had died. Gone was the extra time to perfect his skill with the bow so that he could escape from the tannery pits to glory in war.

'What happened to you?' Her question was soft.

'The monks at the priory taught me some Latin, but I did not want to be a monk. I wanted to see the world. But there was no escape for me either and I...' He was ashamed, even now, to remember. 'I screamed and sulked and kicked and cried and I suspect they were relieved when I ran away.'

He paused. Always astonishing, to think of that journey. From a small boy trapped in the tanning pits to a foot soldier knighted on the field of battle by the Prince himself. Yes, a man could make of himself what he would, as long as he was able-bodied.

And if not...

'And so you will never be trapped yourself.' Her words were rich with understanding.

He wanted to nod, but his head would not move, as if she had trapped him already.

'And you won't,' she said. 'Not by me. I only wanted... something to remember. Nothing has changed. We have only this journey. After that, you will be as free as you were before.'

He nodded, but he was not certain she was right.

But she did not ask again to see his home and he did not take her.

And so the days of the journey rolled by and Anne counted them, finally knowing there were fewer before than behind. When they reached Durham, she could scarcely bear to look at the Cathedral, knowing it would be the last.

Three more days, three more nights until they arrived at Holystone. Would God strike her dead when she crossed the threshold? What was the punishment for such a lie as she had lived? Lady Joan had paid nothing for it, so perhaps it was all for Anne to bear.

Was it a bigger sin than sleeping with Nicholas?

No matter. If death came, she would be content, except that she had never seen Compostela. Or Chartres. Or Rome.

Obviously, God had never intended that she would.

The nights had become more important than the days, but instead of spending that night in Durham making love until dawn, they lay awake, holding each other, as if staying awake might hold back the dawn.

She asked him about his life and listened to the tale of a runaway boy who had become a trusted member of the Prince's retinue.

'And you?' he asked that night. 'You have listened to me for days and told me nothing of your life.'

'My life has been Lady Joan's life.' Not her own. Never her own.

Nicholas leaned on his elbow and raised an eyebrow. 'Lady Joan has had a very interesting life.'

Exactly what she did not want to explore.

If he discovered the truth, he would know she was not a beloved confidante, but only a twisted, damaged liar who had only been kept safe because of the havoc she could wreak.

No. That, she could not let him see. For if he knew who she really was and how she had lied, this fragile thing between them would be gone. And although she had no hope that it would go beyond these days, this brief joy, of a man truly looking into her eyes, the joy of having, even for a moment, a gentle touch, a kiss, a connection that went deeper…ah, that was worth it all. Worth continuing the lie…

She shrugged. 'There is nothing to tell.

'Tell me,' he said, 'how you learned to do needlework.'

Remembrance joined relief. 'I finally had something I could do.' Something that did not need her to be whole. She had missed it during these days of travel. Perhaps she could stitch altar clothes for the nuns. 'It was Salisbury's mother who taught me.'

'His mother?'

She nodded. 'It was shortly after he and Joan were wed. We lived all together then. His father died and I think teaching me gave his mother something to do.'

She had not thought of that in years. Lady Joan's mother had forced the marriage despite her daughter's objections. Circumstances were strained. Salisbury, sixteen and not yet knighted, was suddenly the Earl, struggling to prove himself equal to the task of the title, as well as of being a husband. Meanwhile, his mother grieved over his father and showed Anne how to make her stitches smooth and even.

'So Salisbury was managing all the lands by himself at sixteen?'

'Oh, no. Thomas Holland helped.'

As soon as she said his name, the world become still. A few words. A few seconds. Everything could change. Life could end, just that fast.

'What do you mean?' Nicholas asked.

She could not take the words back, so she must pretend they meant nothing. 'He was the Earl's steward.' This was a fact easily known and discovered, and yet why would anyone even think to ask it? Certainly Nicholas hadn't. Not until now.

She rushed on. 'Holland was not always an Earl. It was through Joan that he received the title.' Did she sound too bright? Too careless? 'He was a squire in the first Earl's retinue. That was why he was in Flanders when he married Joan.'

'But you're not talking about the old Earl now, are you?'

She shook her head.

'When was this? That he worked for his wife's husband?'

How bald it sounded, when he said it. 'I was about eight.'

Nicholas blinked. 'Why would Holland work for a man who had taken his wife? A wife he was trying to claim.'

Could she lie again? Could she tell him she did not remember? Even he would not believe that.

She shrugged. 'Children do not notice such things.'

Even in that, she lied. Children noticed exactly those things. As a child, she had known that the way Lady Joan and the steward had shared touches was meant for a man and his wife.

And why.

Nicholas sat up in the bed and shook his head, certain he had misunderstood. He did not even want to marry, yet he could not have done what either of those men had done. 'If a man had stolen my wife, I would be challenging him on the field of honour, not toiling as his steward. Why would Salisbury hire the man who claimed his wife?'

'Well, he did not know that at the time.' She nodded, lips pursed, and said no more.

He thought he had memorised every detail of the convoluted history of Joan's marriages, but there must have been a gap, something he had missed or forgotten. 'So they marry in Flanders when Joan is twelve, Holland goes off to fight for another three years, then returns to England and works for Salisbury and then waits for three years before he petitions the Pope to restore Joan to him?'

'He didn't have enough money to do so earlier,' she rushed to explain. 'Not until he went to France and captured a prisoner to be ransomed.'

She must misremember. She had only been a child. But the words reminded him of doubts he had

smothered before. Why would a man wait seven years
to claim his rightful wife? Why would Joan have even
agreed to the marriage with Salisbury if she believed
she was already wed?

Worse, why would Holland live with, even serve
the man, day by day, and then watch his own wife go
up to bed with him night after night?

He could not imagine it. No man he knew could
tolerate such a thing. Unless…

Unless he had not been married to her. Unless he
only started sleeping with her himself after he came
to work for her husband and used the clandestine
marriage as an excuse to break a valid marriage and
take her himself.

That explanation looked obvious, now that he
faced it. The story about the secret wedding in Flanders, that could be swallowed. But what man in love
and in the right, with God on his side would return to
find his wife married to another man and after what
must count as a truly perfunctory protest, wait years
to pursue his claim?

What husband brings into his household a man
who claims to have wed his wife?

Anne was looking down at her hands, as if she
wished they were busy with needle and thread. Could
she have known? Had she known all along?

He tried to tell himself no. Tried to tell himself
that she was too young.

My mother was the witness.

And Anne had been with Lady Joan ever since.

He tried to think of another interpretation, but

what had been justified as kindness now seemed like coercion.

And the only way the plan worked was for Anne to know, too. As well as her mother did. Well enough that Lady Joan had to pay her with protection for life.

Yes, Anne's mother had good reason to lie before God and man. To provide for a child that would have no place in the world otherwise.

But now, that child was a liability because she knew the truth of a matter so huge that it would rock the throne of England.

And now, so did he.

'Anne.' His very tone commanded that she meet his eyes and when she did, he saw what he should have recognised all along. 'There was no marriage, was there?'

Chapter Twenty

Anne's lips turned to stone. She could not tell him.
She must not.

'Of course there was! My mother swore it in the
documents before the Pope. Of course it is true!'

And Anne had wanted to believe it. All her life she
had wanted to believe, even when her mother finally
told her the truth.

'How could she?' he said. 'How could she live
with Salisbury knowing her husband slept under the
same roof?'

'I don't know! She just did.'

'You never questioned? Any of it?'

'Why would I?' She had never wanted to. And
until now, until she had known Nicholas, she had
never really understood the enormity of the question. Now, she knew that if Joan had felt for Thomas
Holland what Anne felt for Nicholas, if the desire had
been strong enough to lead them to bind their hands
together, nothing of God or man would have let her
be 'married' to another man.

'No, of course not. You would have had nothing to gain.'

And everything to lose.

And now, she had everything and more, for to confess to Nicholas would be to lose even the small comfort that he had cared for her, at least for these few months. That precious memory would be swept away by his fury.

Strangely, that was what gave her the courage to tell him. He already believed she had lied and he loathed her for it. To admit the truth would not change that, but it would be the only thing that would redeem her in her own eyes.

She lifted her chin and braved his eyes, which were already tinged with disgust. 'And I have nothing to gain now,' she said. Did she owe him the truth? Maybe she owed it to herself. 'But, yes, you are right.'

'When did you know? When did your mother tell you?'

'Not for years. She wanted me to believe as everyone else did.' It was safer, at least, then.

'And she traded her knowledge for your security.'

She nodded. Everything, everything her mother had done, all the lies all her life, all for Anne's own sake. 'I think she finally told me the truth because she feared something might happen. Joan might have a change of heart…'

He made a sound that wasn't a laugh. 'She's known for that, isn't she?'

She felt her anger stir. Until now, Joan had been

kind to her. 'My lady tries always to please people.'
Particularly men.

But sometimes, it was not possible to please one
without angering another. She could not please her
mother and the King and the Queen, who all wanted
her to marry Salisbury, and still keep herself and
Thomas Holland happy.

'Yet she has turned other's lives upside down not
once, but again and again.'

'She took care of me!'

'Because your mother made certain she would!
Because if she didn't, you could destroy her.'

Her lady had sent her north because she feared
just this. The secret she held so dear, as tenderly as a
cherished pet, had become a viper. Now that it was
revealed, Lady Joan would not be the only one poi-
soned.

She could see by his face that Nicholas had just
begun to realise the cascade of implications. 'That
means,' he began, with the quick logic she loved, 'that
she is actually married to Salisbury, and always has
been. There was no marriage to Holland, ever. Their
children are bastards. And…'

He looked at her with growing horror.

She nodded. 'And her marriage to Edward is also
invalid because her husband, Salisbury, her real husband, still lives.'

Numbness came first. Even though Nicholas had
said the words, even though his mind had processed
the facts and they lay, indisputable, before him, sur-

prise had drawn a veil over them, preventing the full impact of the blow from reaching him all at once.

Because the worst thing was not that the Prince had joined with another man's wife. Not that bastards would sit on the throne of England. Not even that, for all his good intentions, he had successfully thwarted God's laws and caused Popes and Archbishops to sanction it.

No, the biggest horror was that he had made his father's mistake all over again. He had let himself be fooled, thinking that a poor cripple needed sympathy. In fact, she had manipulated him like the worst beggar in the street, who whined and begged and, when your back was turned, rose and danced down the street.

He had trusted this woman, even thought to love her, and she had lied. Knew the truth and kept it from him. From all of them.

As his brain struggled to accept the truth, questions, and implications, started to flow.

'But the King,' he continued. 'And the Queen. How could they have stood by and allowed—?'

'They did not.' Her answer was quick and emphatic. 'They believed her story. And once they did…'

Of course. Once the King and Queen accepted the 'truth', who would challenge it?

'The Prince?' He tried to imagine lying beside a woman you loved and not feeling, not somehow knowing. Yet hadn't he done the same? 'Does Edward know?'

She shook her head. 'No.'

'Of course not.' Joan, any woman, obviously, was capable of lying so cleverly that even in lovemaking she could conceal the truth. 'That would not suit Joan's purposes. Nor yours.'

They had plotted to deceive the Prince, the two of them, and made Nicholas an unwitting party to it. Only an accident, a slip of the tongue, had revealed it even now.

He was so angry, he had no shield for it. He grabbed her shoulders and shook her. 'Who else knows?'

'Joan. Me. No one else living.'

Holland and Anne's mother. Now dead.

All this time, he had wondered why she and Joan were so close. Now, he knew. They were locked together by this secret. A secret that kept Anne clothed and fed and off the streets.

And looking at her, he could see why. If Joan had not sheltered Anne after she was orphaned, had not lifted her out of the mud into that rarified air that royalty breathed, she would have died on the street, perhaps. Laughed at or spat on. Forced to dance for the amusement of the peasants, or shunned for her assumed sins.

Ah, there was the truth of life. All were not equal in the sight of God. He created each to his own role. One forgot that to his, or her, peril.

For a moment, he understood. Even…forgave.

No. Not this time.

'You. Lady Joan. And now, me.'

'What will you do?' Strange, that he saw no fear in her eyes.

'Will I tell him? Is that what you mean?'

There should have been no question where his obligation lay, but for a moment, he didn't know the answer. Would he let England's future King ascend, knowing his marriage and his children were invalid? Perhaps he should leave punishment to God.

And what would happen if the secret were exposed? He was not a man learned in the intricacies of canon law, but the only similar case he knew of involved a man who had married two wives. In that case, the wife was forgiven for her ignorance.

No such option existed here.

Anne grabbed his arms. 'What good will the truth do anyone now? How many lives will be upset by the truth?'

'Yours, of course.' Yet for that reason alone, he hesitated and cursed his weakness.

She did not even bother to laugh at that. 'My life is of little consequence.'

'Do you not care that the entire kingdom is wronged by the lie? That the Queen will be a concubine. Worse. A *bigamist?* And her children bastards?'

What calamities might God send all of them as punishment?

For a moment, Anne looked as cynical as he felt. 'It will not be the first time a bastard has sat on England's throne. Do you not care about Joan's children?'

'She and the Prince have no children.' Yet.

'Her children with Thomas Holland. She has four.

Little Joan, Thomas, John, Maud. You saw them. Would you make them bastards without rights to their father's title?'

'It would not be me who makes them so. It would be your lady.' The children were of her body, the fruit of her sin.

'What of Salisbury?' Anne continued relentlessly. Anne, who had known for years of the implications he was only beginning to grasp. 'What of the wife he married when he was forced to release Joan? She is innocent and blameless, as is their son. What of them?'

The litany, the endless list of ruined lives, all because Thomas Holland was no better at controlling his lust than Nicholas's father.

No better than Nicholas himself.

Nicholas rose. Three more days to the convent where he would be rid of her. And then… 'I will sleep elsewhere tonight. We will leave early tomorrow.'

'But…'

'There is nothing you can say I want to hear. Anything you tell me now I will never believe.'

She nodded, slowly, as if she had expected no more from him. She was Anne again, determined to meet the fate life had decreed for her without complaint.

And that was harder for him to bear than if she had pleaded for his silence.

'And tomorrow?'

'Tomorrow, I'll take you on to Holystone and after I leave you there, I'm leaving England. All of you can burn in hell together.'

She struggled to rise and he forced himself not to

help her. He must not touch her again. And when she finally stood straight, legs braced against the bed so she would not fall, she radiated a near-regal air of command. 'Do not take me to the convent. Take me back to court.'

Ah, as he should have known. She would return to Lady Joan so they could plot anew.

He shrugged agreement. Let them. It would do no good. He was going to reveal everything to the Prince. After that? A lifetime of lies would come to an end.

In silence, they retraced country Anne had thought never to see again. This time, she did not savour the sights, nor try to commit the miles to memory.

She told herself she did not grieve to lose Nicholas's love, for she had never thought to win or keep it. But even the brief time with him had given her courage she could never have imagined. The courage to choose.

All her life, she had been told she had no choices. She was crippled and lucky to have Joan's protection, protection she must keep at all costs. Beyond that, she tried to make her foot, even herself, invisible.

But Nicholas never defined her that way. Nor did he use it as an excuse for her. He knew it was a fact of her, was careful and considerate of it, but for the first time, she had met someone who saw something more in her.

More, even, than she had seen in herself.

So now she would not go quietly to a convent, shut away from life for the rest of her days. She would rather spend them begging by the side of the road to the cathedral.

But there was one thing she must do first. In all their years together, their understanding had been unspoken. When her mother told her, she had also warned Anne never to speak of it. So between Anne and her lady, there had been glances and pauses, sentences begun and not completed, but never had Lady Joan acknowledged the truth.

She would now. Anne would make certain of it.

The walls of Windsor surrounded them again, finally, on a cold, grey November afternoon.

Anne had hoped for a word of farewell from Nicholas, but it did not come. At the base of the tower, Nicholas tossed the reins to Eustace and, without a pause, started up the infinite staircase. He would reach the top, she was certain, before she had hobbled a quarter of the way. He would speak with the Prince before she gained the final step.

She sent Agatha ahead and began her climb. No need to hurry now. But by the time Anne reached the pause point three quarters of the way up the staircase, Lady Joan was running toward her, skirt billowing behind her.

There was a window opened to the light here on this small landing and the look of horror on Lady Joan's face told Anne everything she needed to know.

Her lady slowed, took a breath and donned again the false smile. Yet her jaw was tight, her eyes narrow.

Then Anne was wrapped in her arms, surrounded

by a voice, full of concern. 'Anne, what's the matter?
Are you ill? Why have you returned?'

Anne looked into her eyes and saw it, finally, the
thing Lady Joan had hidden for so long.

Fear.

Fear that weakness and foolish decisions, made
when she was a young, headstrong girl, could not lie
buried for ever.

And in that moment, Anne felt, for the first time,
as if she understood her lady. Had she not done the
same? Had she not allowed desire to drive her to succumb to the first, the only man who had ever really
seen her? Strange to share that understanding just
before all would be shattered.

Her lady's fingers flickered over Anne's hair and
her arm, the way she touched a person she wanted
to charm. 'Are you hurt? Did something happen?'

Anne drew herself as straight as her leg allowed,
reaching for the wall as she swayed. The ride had
been long. The stairs steep. 'I am as well as ever, but
something happened, yes.'

She paused, thinking of her next words. She would
not speak of Nicholas, what they had done or what he
knew. What she must do now had nothing to do with
him. He would make his own decision about what to
tell the Prince. She was the one who must confront
Lady Joan. 'I will not go to a convent.'

Joan licked her lips. 'Anne, you know how dear
you are to me.' It was almost amusing, to see Joan
try to swallow her shock. 'I have taken care of you,

kept you close, for all these years, but if convent life
is not suitable…'

'It is not.'

Now Joan was the one who stiffened her spine.
'Then I have nothing to offer you. I cannot—'

'You mean that *I* cannot,' Anne said. 'I cannot join
the household that will be the Queen's.'

Lady Joan's silence told her all she needed to know.
Anne had fooled herself into believing her lady's care
had been genuine, even when she knew there was another reason for it. Clearly, the concern had been no
more than a mask.

And that truth, ah, that was more painful than the
other. 'That is not what I am asking. That is not the
price of silence. The price of silence is the truth.'

'Mind yourself,' Lady Joan said, gripping Anne's
arm. 'The stairs are steep.'

Chapter Twenty-One

Ushered before the Prince, Nicholas wasted no time on pleasantries. 'I've learned something you must know, my lord. It seems—'

Yet Prince Edward, still wearing the smile of a new spouse, clapped an arm around Nicholas's shoulder. 'First, my friend, I must thank you again for all you did. I never even imagined...' He sighed and shook his head. 'How it could be.'

Such joy on his face. He had never seen Edward so. Bliss, Anne had called it. The same look he had seen on his father's face. The same look he must have worn for those few days with Anne.

An illusion, just as it had been with his father.

'Can I not persuade you, Nicholas, to find a wife instead of leaving for war again?'

'I am not a man meant for domestic things.'

'I thought I was not either. Until my Jeanette.'

Ah, he wore a smile any man would envy. And Nicholas, to his regret, was about to destroy it.

He tried again. 'Edward, you knew of Joan's past, that she was no maiden.' This speech, rehearsed as all the others, still would not come. 'You knew and yet…'

'Yet I gave up everything for a woman known for her amorous nature as well as for her beauty?'

'You put it bluntly.'

'And you wonder why. Well, my friend, some day you may meet a woman for whom you will be willing to do the most ridiculous things.'

'How can you know the truth of someone?' Or could you ever? And what must you do when you do know?

The Prince shrugged. 'You are the one who figures things out, Nicholas. I'm the one who follows my feelings. That is all I did.'

Followed his feelings. Exactly what had got him, all of them, into trouble. A good reminder. He must not weaken now. He must speak. 'Edward, I must tell you something about Joan. Something—'

'Nicholas.' The word was a statement. 'There is nothing you can tell me about Joan that would make a difference.'

'But…' But as he saw the stubborn set of Edward's jaw, Nicholas let the sentence fade.

'Nothing.' Finality, certainty, in one word.

And he thought, perhaps, that Anne had been wrong when she said the Prince did not know. Perhaps Joan *had* told him. Or told him enough that he should have known…

Whatever he knew, he did not want to know more.

Nicholas sighed. 'Sometimes it turns out badly.'

'It won't. Not for me.'

Because he was a Prince? Because he had been touched by greatness his whole life? Or maybe because he refused to let anything, even his duty, intrude on his happiness.

Because sometimes, foolish emotions could lead to bliss instead of entrapment.

And all the arguments he had clung to all his life seemed nothing more than resentment that a man and a woman should be happy together. He had not believed it possible. And yet, perhaps his father had been content, happy even. Nicholas was the unhappy one who had kicked and screamed, resenting something that had nothing, really, to do with him.

All these years, Nicholas had refused to let himself be happy because he had carried the resentment with him, dragged it wherever he went, just like Anne's lame foot, making him unable to move toward something, only to run away.

No, he would not be the one to destroy the man's happiness because of his own disbelief. God, not Nicholas Lovayne, would mete out punishment, if punishment were due to Edward or Joan or to the kingdom itself. Let them live with their choices. And let Thomas Holland's children, and Salisbury's, live in the bliss of ignorance.

He forced his attention back to Edward, who was speaking to him still.

'You did all I asked of you and more,' Edward was saying. 'Now, there is something I want to do for you. Since you insist on returning to the Continent, I'm going to make it easier for you. I will assume responsibility for your hostage. When the gold comes from France to free him, it will come to me, in repayment for this.'

He laid a pouch of coins, heavy, in Nicholas's hand. He stared at it, seeing all the freedom he had ever wanted.

'There. Enjoy your life of freedom.'

Freedom.

He had spent his life, it seemed, running from things that might require commitment, preferring the temporary to the lasting. Ready to die rather than savour and enjoy the life he had been given.

And he never realised it until Anne.

Anne. He must tell her he had kept the secret before she told Lady Joan everything.

He turned, abruptly. 'There's something else I must do.'

Lady Joan's fingers pinched Anne's arm, throwing Anne off balance. She reached for the wall and shifted her weight away from the stair's edge.

One stumble and she would tumble down near two hundred steps to certain death.

'The truth,' Anne began, 'is that there was no betrothal in Flanders.'

Joan was deadly white. 'What do you mean?'

'All these years. The story my mother told about you and Thomas making a marriage vow. It is a lie.'

'Whatever makes you say that?'

But she does not deny it. 'Because it is the truth.'

'You should not even suggest such a thing.' Even though they were alone, Lady Joan looked over her shoulder. 'Who have you told?'

There was power in questions now, not in making answers. 'Did you even know him in Flanders?'

'Of course I did. Your mother found us, we pledged ourselves before God…'

Perhaps in trying to please Holland and Salisbury and God, Lady Joan remembered only what she wished the truth to be, had lived the lie so long that she had come to believe it herself.

'Mother told me there was no commitment. No marriage.'

'And you believed that?' Wide-eyed with surprise. 'To think you have carried such an awful, wicked thought all these years! If you had come to me, asked me, I would have told you the truth. We did marry.' Her fists clenched now. 'We did.'

Anne shook her head. 'But everything you have done, taking care of me all my life, that was repayment because my mother kept your secret.'

'But I have known you, loved you, since you were a child, Anne. That is why I care for you now, no other reason.'

Doubts of a lifetime crowded in on her. 'But Mother told me. She told me that she had lied for you. And that the price was that you would see that I was cared for after she was gone.'

Lady Joan patted her arm, gently. The look of fear had turned to one of compassion. 'And now you ask me if it is true because you doubt what she told you.

As you should. There was a marriage. She did witness it. She attested the same to the Pope himself. Your mother would never have committed such a sin as to lie to His Holiness.'

Doubt whispered to her. Could her mother have lied to her instead of to the Pope? She searched her mind for something, anything, that might tell her what was false and what was true.

Of Flanders, when she was four, Anne remembered nothing. And when Thomas Holland had come to Salisbury, well, she had been right about one thing. Children didn't always notice, or understand, what they did see.

But being a woman in love, that Anne now understood. 'If you married Holland in April, how could you marry Salisbury before winter was over? Months. It was only months.'

After only one night Anne knew she would remember Nicholas all her days.

But it had been only a few months after Thomas Holland died that Lady Joan joined hands with the Prince of Wales in a darkened chapel at Windsor Castle.

Now Joan whispered, words from the darkness of memory. 'My parents owed Salisbury a debt. They wanted the union so much and I thought, well…they convinced me.'

Joan, always wanting to please others.

But she had walked into the past now and found remembered anger. 'And Thomas had left me! Off to Prussia to fight the heathens without even thinking of me.' She sighed. 'But when he returned from the wars, when I saw him again, I knew I was his wife in God's eyes. And he asserted it, too, demanded I be returned to him.'

'Really? To whom did he make this demand?'

'To my husband. To the Queen. To the King. But they wouldn't listen, not even to me, when I told them the same.'

Her husband. Was that a slip of the tongue? 'Did you tell them?' Anne had trouble picturing Lady Joan arguing with the King and Queen.

'Of course. You remember. You were there.'

Anne searched her memory, but she had been only five, still too young to wonder what went on when the adults closed their doors. 'But Holland ploughed on anyway.' Anne felt a bite of jealousy. No matter what her sins, Lady Joan had had men mad with love for her. Anne still envied her that.

'Until he had enough money to pursue the dissolution. That was when Salisbury locked me in the tower.'

Anne remembered that, of course, for it was a few years later and she was near maiden age herself. Salisbury, a sensible man, probably thought that if he removed his wife from temptation, she, easily swayed, would come to her senses.

And perhaps she would have, if Holland had stepped aside again. Or if Anne's mother had not gone to visit the Pope...

'So you see?' Joan turned back, her calm tone carrying the finality of a conversation's end. 'There was no great secret. It is all as the world knows. I was married to Thomas. Your mother's lies must not trouble you.'

All the pieces could fit, when Lady Joan had explained them, except...

'No. That could not be the way it happened.' Nearly six years had passed between Thomas Holland's return from Prussia and his petition to the Pope. Years in which he served both the elder and the younger Earls of Salisbury. 'If Thomas Holland claimed to be your husband before God, why would Salisbury retain him as a steward? How could they fight beside each other against the French?'

Nicholas was right. It could not be believed.

'Thomas was a knight,' Lady Joan began, with an edge of panic in her voice. 'I was the granddaughter of a King, married to an Earl.' Her voice rose as she rattled off all the reasons. All the excuses. 'The King would not support his petition for me so Thomas knew he could not be successful in the English courts and he had no money to take the case to the Pope, not at first, not until he captured a Count in France and received a ransom.'

Still not to be believed. 'So Salisbury kept him as part of the household, even paid him money that he must have known would go toward taking you away from him?'

'It was the only way we could be together.'

Words, finally, with the ring of truth. A passionate few months in Flanders forgotten until Thomas returned. And with him, Lady Joan's hunger.

Her mother had been right.

'But he wasn't your husband, was he?' Anne said in a whisper. 'He was a strong soldier and you a young maiden and you knew him in Flanders, yes. Knew him carnally because he swept you off your feet and into his bed. And my mother found you together, just as she always said. That much was true.'

Silence from her lady. No denials now. Only an expression of horror, as she saw her life dismembered before her eyes.

'But there was no promise, was there? Not then. Not in Flanders. It was only later, when you saw him again, when he was in your household every day. Much older and stronger than your husband, who was still near a boy.'

It felt freeing, to speak so. As if she were running on two good legs.

'You know nothing. I loved him. And I gave up that love for what I was told was duty. You wouldn't understand.'

'Ah, but I do.' She smiled and, for a moment, they were equals, women who had done foolish things for love.

Anne saw then, suddenly, that she had tried so hard not to let her lameness define her life. Fought against the physical limitations and the attitudes. But on the other hand, she had let it define her life totally. Had given herself over to Joan's keeping because she had thought there was no other choice. And had been made to feel grateful when all the time it was Lady Joan who should have been grateful.

She lifted her head. She was taking her life back now and she would return her lady's life, as well. 'The secret is mine no longer. I return it to you. The truth is your burden, not mine. But that means I am free. And so are you. You need not care for me any longer.'

'Free?' Joan's face had screwed into an expression Anne had never seen, twisted like a gargoyle. 'Without me, you will be free to beg with your bowl and your deformed foot.'

Strangely, the thought did not frighten her. 'All,' she said, a slow smile taking her mouth, 'all will be as it must.'

Something in Joan's face snapped. 'Yes, it will. I gave you a choice. You should have taken it.'

And it wasn't until then that Anne realised they were alone and saw how far down it was to the bottom of the stairs.

And how easy it would be to fall.

Nicholas came to the Tower stairs only after he had searched everywhere else. Both Lady Joan and Anne were missing, as he expected, conspiring together, perhaps, about what to do now that the secret had been shared.

And there they were, on a landing partway down. But they were not standing with heads together. Anne was too near the edge of the step. Lady Joan reached out, but instead of pulling her to safety, she pushed…

No. Not now. Not now that I know…

First, Nicholas froze, heart, brain, legs, nothing

moving as Anne slipped off the step and slid down the stairs.

Then he plunged down the steps.

Heedless of his own footing, he skipped stairs, trusting he would hit the next tread without looking down, looking only at Anne.

She reached for a hold and when that failed, pulled her arms in, so that she was rolling on her side, over and over. Her crutch, no help now, clattered wildly behind her, racing her to the bottom.

Hopeless, really, to think he could run faster than she could fall. The woman he could lightly lift on and off the horse seemed to hurtle toward the bottom, rolling over and over, with the speed of an arrow shot from a longbow.

He caught up with her when she reached the landing, halfway down, and lay on her back, motionless. Afraid to move her, Nicholas shielded her with his body, willing her to be alive.

Then he felt her breath against his cheek and sent up a prayer of thanks.

And then he wondered. What if she had broken bones, a leg or an arm? Worse, her neck or her back? What if she could not move or walk or hold her crutch?

He leaned away so he could see her. 'Anne. Anne.' He ran his hands quickly over her arms and legs. 'Do you hurt? Are you all right?'

She nodded. Her neck worked, then. 'Nicholas?' Then she glanced up and he followed her gaze. Lady

Joan was running down the stairs, her face a mask of concern.

She joined them, her skirt covering Nicholas's arm, and crouched down, stroking a hair away from Anne's white forehead. 'Anne? Are you all right?' Then she looked to Nicholas. 'Thank goodness you were here. It's so awkward for her, yet she insists. As if she will not let her leg hold her back.' She turned back. 'Anne?'

'Yes.' A soft and painful word. She closed her eyes again.

The Princess took a breath. It did not seem to be one of relief. 'Come. Bring her to my chambers. I don't want her trying to walk. Not now.'

'No!' Anne's voice had the steel in it he knew so well. 'It is too much trouble.'

The Prince's wife rose and looked down on them with the imperial gaze of a woman now part of the royal family. 'I insist. Bring her.'

'Please. Let me rest here, just for a bit.' Anne's fingers dug into his arm, hidden where Joan could not see.

Joan. Joan, who had pushed Anne when she thought they were alone. When Anne had returned unexpectedly from exile.

Fool. He had misjudged the situation entirely.

Suddenly, he wondered whether Anne was the only one in danger.

And he wondered whether this time, he would be able to find a way out.

Chapter Twenty-Two

Anne had thought him an angel at first. Thought she had woken in Purgatory, where she would pay for her sins.

Yet she still lived, breathed, and lay near Nicholas again. One more memory to hold. The feel of his arms, strong around her one final time. It seemed, now, that she might not have years left to think back on it.

If Lady Joan had her way, Anne might have hours.

'The Prince was looking for you,' Nicholas said, the words comforting above her.

Her lady's face changed. 'Where is he?'

'I'm not certain. He was near the Hall when I left him.'

She rose. 'Take Anne to my quarters where she can be cared for. I'll be there as soon as I can. Leave her stick here. She won't need it.'

Nicholas waited until Lady Joan had disappeared at the top of the stairs, then he retrieved her stick.

She wondered why he was here. Ah, because the Prince had sent him to find her lady. That was her good fortune, these extra minutes. 'May your journey be safe.' Nonsense, but the shock of the fall and then the shock of seeing him had turned the world on edge. 'Remember to look at the cathedrals as well as the battlefields.'

He didn't answer, but touched her methodically, searching for parts in pain, and when he opened his mouth, what came out was not what she expected. 'Can you move at all?'

She would be black and blue for weeks, but God had been merciful. Nothing seemed to be broken. She nodded and he helped her sit upright.

'Are you dizzy?'

She shook her head, grateful that she could.

'How do you feel?'

Free. I feel free. 'Lady Joan…' she could not tell him she was in danger. That would put him in danger, too '…worries overmuch.'

Could she manage to escape Windsor before Lady Joan found her? She would not be so lucky the next time.

'No more lies, Anne. She pushed you. I saw her.'

She met his eyes. No, there was no reason to lie. He knew all the truths. 'In all these years, she had never said anything. Never admitted anything. It was as if we both knew, but we never said a word. I wanted her to admit the truth.'

'What did she say?'

'That my mother had lied to me, not to the Pope.

I wonder what she will say when the Prince confronts her.'

'I did not tell him.'

She stared at him. 'What?'

'Oh, I tried. But he did not want to know. Or did not want to admit that he already knew. Your lady's secret is safe.'

She smiled and shook her head. All the years. All this time.

Nicholas was not smiling. 'You, however, are not. If you feel well enough to move, I'm taking you away from here before she kills you.'

Nicholas had no time to explain, no time to do anything beyond act to keep her safe. Fortunately, Anne did not argue. The habits of his life, planning, finding alternate routes, continuing to move, all those worked to get them out of Windsor and on the road.

He left a message saying Anne had decided to return to the convent and pray for the remainder of her life. He only hoped Lady Joan would believe it. Or if she chose to search, that she would send the men north instead of east. He smuggled her out in a cart, which not only made it easier to hide her, but also allowed her to sleep for long stretches of the journey. She might not have broken anything, but, bruised and shaken, she needed time to heal.

Anne had asked few questions, made no complaints, and Nicholas hadn't wasted breath to discuss the future until they were days and miles away. By then, she could sit up in the cart and move without wincing and on the fifth day, when they had stopped to eat by the road side, he had found himself staring at her. Something had transformed her. No, her leg had not healed, but something that had dragged down her face for all those years had lifted when she walked away from Joan. Homeless and without protection, she looked radiant.

After they ate, she pulled out her pilgrim's badge, the one he had given her, and ran her fingers over the outline of Saint Thomas' horse. 'How far are we from Canterbury?' she said.

'Maybe five days.'

'Will you take me there?'

This part he had not planned. 'Do you believe the Saint will cure you?' When it did not happen immediately, many pilgrims stayed near, in faith that the cure would come in time. Sometimes it did. Sometimes, death came instead.

'No. But I think it is a good choice. At least for now. I believe I now have a choice.'

'I would offer you a different choice,' he said.

She looked puzzled. 'What would that be? Not the convent.'

He smiled. 'Nothing like the convent. Come with me.'

Anne's heart beat in her ears so loudly she thought she must have misheard. She looked at him, unable to hide the sliver of hope, but she would not be the burden that would hold him back. Never.

'With you? Across the Channel? You have not made such a mockery of me before.'

'I do not now. I want you to come with me.'

She shook her head, wondering if the fall had clouded her hearing. 'You want to go back to war and ride freely where it takes you.' And how she envied him that.

'I want you.'

Had her fall ignited his pity? 'There is no place for a crippled woman in that life.'

'But there is room for you.'

She looked at him, not speaking, but knowing all her love for him was in her eyes. 'For me? To do what?'

'I want you, I want us, to go to Compostela, to Rome, to Jerusalem if you like.'

Us. 'There will be no miracle cure from God. Did we not learn that already?'

'Did God not just give us a miracle?'

Her laugh escaped then, the laugh that had saved her from anger and despair so many times. The laugh that reminded her that God's kindness could be cruel and inexplicable. And his cruelty full of mercy. She had taken a fall that could have, should have, killed or at least maimed her. And God had insisted she stay alive. 'Not the one I expected, but, yes.'

'Anne.' He put his hands on her arms. 'Look at me. Please.'

She did, then, intending to take a last picture for her memories. Of his square face with the broad brow, deep-set eyes and lips she only knew were sensual after he had kissed her. 'I'm looking at the man who had said he was leaving England and leaving her to burn in hell.'

'Marry me.'

Did she blink? Did her jaw drop open? Did she nearly fall, held up only by his arms? She licked her lips and swallowed, then started to argue. 'I thought we were beyond pity.' No hope. She mustn't hope. 'Is that what this is about? Do you feel sorry for the poor, helpless cripple?'

'Helpless?' He squeezed her upper arms and gave her a little shake. 'You are the strongest woman—no, strongest person I've ever known. You put Edward's knights to shame.'

The words stopped her speech, this time with heat in her cheeks. 'I thank you for that, but it changes nothing. You cannot have the life you want with me.'

'I cannot have the life I want without you.'

Hope, hope buzzed in her ear, persistent as a fly. 'Are you sure?'

'I love you. I don't want a life without you. I want to take you to all the cathedrals in every city in the whole world. I want to see them, to see everything anew through your eyes. I want to sleep beside you every night and wake beside you every morning. I want to show you the things you need to show me.'

She nearly laughed, then. 'How fanciful you sound.'

'I will help you walk. You can help me see.' His voice, low, his words, intense. 'If you love me, Anne. Please. Come.'

And suddenly, it seemed as if God had indeed given her the miracle she asked for. 'Yes. No matter what, yes.'

They reached Dover the next day. He had sent Eustace by a different way and now he was reunited with his armour and his destrier. Nicholas found a boat willing to brave a winter crossing. Staying longer in England would tempt fate and tempt Lady Joan, too. Eustace would come with them as far as the Continental port. The young man had a taste for war, not pilgrimage. He would go on to find the Great Company and earn his spurs.

'The crossing may be difficult.' Only madmen crossed the Channel in winter. They had braved frost on the road. The winds had picked up.

Yet Anne looked up at him, smiling, happy. 'I've crossed the Channel before. A rocking ship is a good match for my unsteady legs.'

He smiled and put his arms around her, glancing behind to see that they were casting off.

'Don't look back,' she said, looking steadfastly forwards toward Calais and the future.

'It will take months, you know.' Compostela first. A pilgrimage of penance, in case God had wanted them to tell the truth.

'Months by your side to see the world. What else might I hope for?'

'A child.' He did not ask a question, but he watched her face, uncertain what she might say.

The enormity of it was reflected there, followed

by a moment of peace. 'If it comes,' she said, 'I will make my way. With you by my side.'

'As my wife.' A word that sounded wonderful to his ear.

A moment of distress passed across her face. 'How are we to marry? We'll be strangers to a French church. How can they read the banns? What priest would agree?'

He smiled. 'We need none of that.' The boat had pushed off and already the chop was starting, the stiff breeze whipping their hair and cloaks behind them. 'We know exactly what is needed if we are to be wed.'

He reached out and took her hand. 'I, Nicholas, take thee, Anne, to be my wedded wife.'

Her smile became a laugh. 'I, Anne, take thee, Nicholas…'

And the gulls were their witnesses.

* * * * *

Afterword

The accepted wisdom of the clandestine marriages of Joan of Kent is that she did, indeed, marry Thomas Holland, then William Montacute (also Montague), who became the second Earl of Salisbury, and that when Holland returned, he claimed her as his wife by their previous vow. He waited five years to pursue his legal claim to her, however, ostensibly because he lacked money to take it to the courts. After several years, and a petition to the Pope, his claim was accepted and her marriage to Salisbury was put aside.

The story was, apparently, accepted at the time and few questions have been raised about it over the years, though there were whispers. The reference to Joan as the 'Virgin of Kent,' was taken straight from the medieval chronicles. When her son, Richard II, was deposed, he was slurred as a bastard, though that is easily explained as further justification for removing him from the throne.

But as I dug into the details, I could not reconcile

the facts as I uncovered them with the story that had been spun about them.

Why would Joan allow herself to be married if she believed she was already married in God's eyes?

How could her first husband work for her second, and fight beside him, if he were truly married to Joan? And how could Salisbury allow it if Holland had immediately stated his claim when he returned to England in the winter of 1341–42?

Bit by bit, I came to believe that there was another story, more believable, to me, at least, to explain what had happened. It is that story, and its discovery, that drive Nicholas and Anne in this book.

I am not the first modern researcher to raise doubts about Joan's first marriage. Chris Given-Wilson and Alice Curteis in *The Royal Bastards of Medieval England* said much the same thing. There has been no full-scale biography written of Joan, but the scholarly articles continue to support the official story that she had two clandestine marriages.

And what about King Edward and Queen Philippa's role in all this? Joan was in their care when young, so if the story were true, she had 'married' Holland right under the Queen's nose in Flanders. They supported her marriage to Salisbury and one explanation for Holland's long delay in petitioning to have her returned was that he needed the money to go directly to the Pope because the King would have stopped him if he had started with the English ecclesiastical courts, as would have been the protocol. This suggested, to me at least, that Edward did not believe he was in the right. Still, Holland was one of the first knights to be initiated into the Order of the Garter, so he was certainly part of the King's trusted circle.

Imagine King Edward and Queen Philippa's chagrin to have to deal with Joan's irregular marriages not once, but twice, and the second time to their oldest son and future King. A few historians have suggested that the King was opposed to this marriage, but other interpretations disagree and, in the end, he did not forbid it.

And there was a real Nicholas Lovayne—or Loveign or Loveyne or Lovagne—who was sent by the crown to the Curia on matters relating to the dissolution of Joan's marriage not once, but twice. (I have borrowed his name in homage, but few other particulars of his life.) So if King Edward had protested, he ultimately supported his son's efforts.

The traditional tale of the Black Prince and Joan, the Fair Maid of Kent, is that theirs was a love match. It's even been suggested that he had loved his 'Jeanette' as a child and there's a charming, though probably imaginary, tale that the Prince had been sent to plead on behalf of a friend for the hand of the beautiful and wealthy widow. She declined, saying there was only one man she loved and would marry. Him.

Edward and Joan stayed happily married, apparently, for the remainder of Edward's life. Shortly after their marriage, they went to Aquitaine to rule over what was left of Edward III's French possessions. Prince Edward continued his record of successful leadership in war, but died before his father. Thus,

Joan, the first Princess of Wales, never became Queen of England. She was, however, very influential in the court of her son, Richard II, and popular with the people.

After Edward's death, she did not remarry, though she lived another nine years. But on her death she was buried, as she had asked, not beside her royal husband, but 'near the monument of our late lord and husband, the Earl of Kent.' Thomas Holland.

Readers of my other books might want to note these connections. Joan and Thomas's ostensible rendezvous in Flanders took place in the same world as *INNOCENCE UNVEILED,* though I do not portray any of these characters in that story except for Queen Philippa. *THE HARLOT'S DAUGHTER* and *IN THE MASTER'S BED* both take place in the reign of Richard II, Joan's son. She was very likely at court at this time, though again, I did not show her in the story.

Coming soon
WHISPERS AT COURT

Next, Anne's friend Lady Cecily
is drawn to a French knight,
held captive at the English court.

Lady Cecily frowns on the developing romance between the English Princess she serves and a wealthy French lord, held hostage in her father's court. Though King Edward triumphed in war, Cecily's father was slain in battle. The royal family may forgive their one-time enemies. She never will.

Another hostage, Marc de Marcel, resents the English as much as Cecily does the French. Refusing to languish in a foreign land waiting for a ransom that may never be paid, he is determined to find another way home. One his captors will not like. But as Cecily and Marc struggle against an attraction neither wants they discover that love has a way of upsetting the strongest loyalties. And the best-laid plans.

REQUEST YOUR FREE BOOKS!

HARLEQUIN® HISTORICAL:
Where love is timeless

2 FREE NOVELS PLUS 2 **FREE GIFTS!**

YES! Please send me 2 FREE Harlequin® Historical novels and my 2 FREE gifts (gifts are worth about $10). After receiving them, if I don't wish to receive any more books, I can return the shipping statement marked "cancel." If I don't cancel, I will receive 6 brand-new novels every month and be billed just $5.44 per book in the U.S. or $5.74 per book in Canada. That's a savings of at least 16% off the cover price! It's quite a bargain! Shipping and handling is just 50¢ per book in the U.S. and 75¢ per book in Canada.* I understand that accepting the 2 free books and gifts places me under no obligation to buy anything. I can always return a shipment and cancel at any time. Even if I never buy another book, the two free books and gifts are mine to keep forever.

246/349 HDN F4ZY

Name _____ (PLEASE PRINT) _____

Address _____ Apt. # _____

City _____ State/Prov. _____ Zip/Postal Code _____

Signature (if under 18, a parent or guardian must sign) _____

Mail to the **Harlequin® Reader Service:**
IN U.S.A.: P.O. Box 1867, Buffalo, NY 14240-1867
IN CANADA: P.O. Box 609, Fort Erie, Ontario L2A 5X3
Want to try two free books from another line?
Call 1-800-873-8635 or visit www.ReaderService.com.

* Terms and prices subject to change without notice. Prices do not include applicable taxes. Sales tax applicable in N.Y. Canadian residents will be charged applicable taxes. Offer not valid in Quebec. This offer is limited to one order per household. Not valid for current subscribers to Harlequin Historical books. All orders subject to credit approval. Credit or debit balances in a customer's account(s) may be offset by any other outstanding balance owed by or to the customer. Please allow 4 to 6 weeks for delivery. Offer available while quantities last.

Your Privacy—The Harlequin® Reader Service is committed to protecting your privacy. Our Privacy Policy is available online at www.ReaderService.com or upon request from the Harlequin Reader Service.

We make a portion of our mailing list available to reputable third parties that offer products we believe may interest you. If you prefer that we not exchange your name with third parties, or if you wish to clarify or modify your communication preferences, please visit us at www.ReaderService.com/consumerschoice or write to us at Harlequin Reader Service Preference Service, P.O. Box 9062, Buffalo, NY 14269. Include your complete name and address.

HH13R

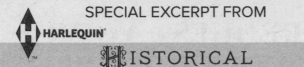
Next month, get swept away by Rhys Denham and Lady Thea as they embark on a journey of adventure, passion and discovery…

Rhys sighed and moved his mouth gently against the head of the woman in his arms. This was the way to wake up. Warm, rocking gently, arms full of soft, curvaceous femininity.

She smelled of roses, whoever she was. He must try to recall her name in a minute; it was ungentlemanly to forget in the morning. Not that he could recall the night before either, but he supposed it must have been good. His body was certainly awake and interested.

When he pulled her more tightly against him she snuggled back with an erotic little wriggle that inflamed him to aching point.

"Mmm." Rhys nuzzled the silky-fine hair and let his right hand stray lightly across her body. They were both dressed, after a fashion, although their bare feet had obviously made friends in the night. Perhaps she had pulled on her gown again afterward for warmth, because under the fine wool he could feel uncorseted curves and the sweet weight of an unfettered breast. As his thumb moved across the nipple it hardened, and he smiled.

His companion stirred, stretched, her feet sliding down against his. She yawned and he came completely awake. He was in the chaise, on the ship, heading for France, and in his arms, pressed against him, her breast cupped in his hand, was Lady Althea Curtiss.

Rhys bit back the word that sprang to his lips and went very still. Was she awake? Had she realized? Probably not or she'd be screaming the place down or, given that this was Thea, applying that sharp elbow where it would do most harm. He let his hand fall away from her breast, lifted the other from her hip and arched his midsection as far back as he could. If he tried to slide his arm from under her she would probably wake.

Damn it. *Thea,* the innocent, respectable friend whom he had already shocked with that embrace.

Rhys thought about Almack's, tripe and onions, Latin verbs, tailors' accounts. It didn't work. His brain, apparently having lost all its blood in a mad southward dash, was disobediently musing on just where Thea had acquired those curves from and when she had begun to smell of roses and how that mousy mane of hair could be so silky.

"Rhys?" His name was muffled in a yawn.

Don't miss
UNLACING LADY THEA by Louise Allen
available from Harlequin® Historical April 2014.

HISTORICAL

Where love is timeless

COMING IN APRIL 2014

Welcome to Wyoming
by Kate Bridges

Seeking justice for his murdered colleagues, Detective Simon Garr
has gone undercover as infamous jewel thief Jarrod Ledbetter.
All is going to plan, until he finds out that Jarrod's mail-order
bride is on her way to Wyoming! Simon can't afford to jeopardize
his cover, and he's left with only one option—he must marry
the woman!

When his poor bride Natasha O'Sullivan arrives she doesn't have
a clue what she is walking into—but Simon finds there is more to
her than first meets the eye. Because Natasha has brought along
secrets of her own....

Mail-Order Weddings
From blushing bride to Wild West wife!

Available wherever books and ebooks are sold.

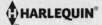

HARLEQUIN®

HISTORICAL
Where love is timeless

The Wedding Ring Quest
by Carla Kelly

Penniless Mary Rennie knows she's lucky to have a home in Edinburgh, but she does crave more excitement in her life. So when her cousin's ring is lost in one of several fruitcakes heading around the country as gifts, Mary seizes the chance for adventure.

When widowed captain Ross Rennie and his son meet Mary in a coaching inn, they take her under their wing. After years of battling Napoleon, Ross's soul is war-weary, but Mary's warmth and humor touch him deep inside. Soon, he's in the most heart-stopping situation of his life—considering a wedding-ring quest of his own!

Coming in April 2014

Available wherever books and ebooks are sold.

HH29781